Worlds Apart

A science-fiction novel

Written by

Fay Smith

PublishAmerica
Baltimore

ISBN: 1-4241-5140-6
PUBLISHED BY PUBLISHAMERICA, LLLP
www.publishamerica.com
Baltimore

Printed in the United States of America

Acknowledgements

For my family. Especially my husband, Hank, whose encouragement kept me going. And to my mother, LeNora Conkle, the author of five books, who inspired me to start writing.

A special thanks to my Advanced Writing Class for their input and valued critiquing.

CHARACTERS AND LOCATIONS

BOSTONIA: CAPITAL OF NEW EARTH
KARDON FAUS: PREFECT OF NEW EARTH
   (ASSASSINATED)
BARDAS VANTRA: PRINCE OF NEW EARTH
BORCRONS: PRINCE VANTRA'S ELITE GUARDS
RYDEN CALDAR: JESSICA'S FATHER (A SCIENTIST)
JESSICA CALDAR: A CHASER FOR THE FEDERATION
LEGEND: COMPUTER OF ARTIFICIAL INTELLIGENCE
NAAL & PROTANDEL: MERCENARIES HIRED
   TO KIDNAP JESSICA
ACRONON-FIVE: OUTLAW PLANET
QUAD: CHIEF OF NEW EARTH'S CHASERS
AUGUEEN: QUAD'S WIFE
CONDEE & RETSEL: QUAD'S SONS
BORKIA: QUAD AND AUGUEEN'S HOME PLANET
PRAGORA: COLONY ON PLANET ZEER
JAROD KRINNER: A CHASER ON PRAGORA
KRAFT TAYBOR: FLIGHT COMMANDER ON PRAGORA
ETERNIANS: AWAITING A NEW MILLENNIA
ANCIENTS: GUARDIANS OF ETERNA
KELL: AN ANDROID
CRYSTAL CAVES: WHERE ETERNIANS ARE
   IMPRISONED
RAZZOON: GUARDIAN OF THE "PROPHECY"
MYRA: AN ETERNIAN

TIME LINE

2225	THE EARTH IS DECIMATED BY ASTEROID SHOWER
2340	COLONISTS RETURN TO BUILD NEW EARTH
2392	CONSTRUCTION BEGINS ON NEW EARTH'S CAPITAL, BOSTONIA
2427	OLD CAPITAL IS DISCOVERED
3132	JAROD KRINNER IS BORN
3135	JESSICA CALDAR IS BORN
3132 – 3144	KORDON FAUS IS PREFECT OF NEW EARTH
3142	PLANETS SPLIT FROM NEW EARTH'S GOVERNMENT
3144	KORDON FAUS IS ASSASSINATED
3145	BARDAS VANTRA TAKES HIS PLACE AS PREFECT
3148	BARDAS VANTRA BRINGS PEACE TO THE GALAXY (BECOMES PRINCE OF NEW EARTH) (THE AGE OF "ENLIGHTENMENT")
3148	ETERNIANS REBEL (JESSICA IS 13)
3149	JAROD KRINNER IS SENT TO ETERNA TO BE TRAINED (AGE 17)
3152	JESSICA CALDAR BECOMES A CHASER (AGE 17)
3252	JAROD KRINNER ARRIVES ON ZEER, BECOMES A CHASER FOR PRAGORAIAN COLONY (AGE 20)
3153	JESSICA'S FATHER, RYDEN CALDAR, IS KILLED (JESSICA IS 18)
3159	PRESENT: (JESSICA IS 24 – JAROD IS 27)

In the year 3142 all but four of the galactic planets and their satellites split from New Earth's governing power. Those choosing to remain were Moon Base Andromeda, Jupiter, Saturn, and Mars colony Tros. New Earth's Prefect, Kordon Faus, was assassinated two years later, leaving New Earth in great upheaval. His successor, a charismatic leader named Bardas Vantra, formed a galactic peace treaty with the warring planets, and through sheer power declared himself Prince of New Earth.

With his power came change and not all to the good. Bostonia, the capital city of New Earth, was the first to embrace THE ENLIGHTENMENT; Vantra's world order of knowledge without God. One by one New Earth's sixty-three colonies acknowledged his supremacy and followed suit. The destruction of all religious books was ordered, stating they were an impediment; relics of an age humanity no longer needed. The ancient religions exchanged their faith for power and knowledge. Science became their god. However, not all chose to follow this new cult. The Eternians rebelled. Though outnumbered, with few weapons and many enemies, they bravely fought on, but defeat came swiftly. With the help of Chasers, Prince Vantra's BorCrons rounded up the dissenters and shipped them to the abandoned crystal mining caves of Pragora, on the planet Zeer.

Six years prior to this rebellion, Ryden Caldar, one of New Earth's greatest scientists, secretly developed a computer of artificial intelligence whom he named Legend. Jessica, his daughter, sharing his secret, will fulfill her father's dream as well as her own destiny.

Prologue

"You've been helping to transport Eternians to another planet!" Prince Vantra raged, pointing his finger at the near unconscious man before him. "Did you think you could keep me from finding out about the portal? You're a fool, Ryden, I have spies everywhere."

Pacing back and forth, Vantra's face was cold and rigid. "I knew they were dangerous, and you're one of them." Turning to the mercenary he had hired, Vantra shouted, "Get on with it!"

Ryden Caldar slumped backward in the steel chair, his hands bound behind him. He blinked several times, trying to bring into focus the man standing over him, arm upraised to strike again and again. Blood gushed from Ryden's nose and mouth; his head rolled sideways wrenching a groan from his lacerated lips. A spasm racked his body. Darkness enveloped Ryden's soul and the room faded away.

Chapter 1
Assignment

Legend signaled an incoming call. "Shall I transfer it to my monitor?" he inquired of Jessica.

"No, I better take it on the house visual," she replied. Exiting the lab, she strode into her office and switched on the visual. Instantly the stormy face of Quad flashed onto the monitor. "What's up, chief? Must be important for you to call me at home."

"Prince Vantra's disappeared and the Council is in an uproar!" Quad started to pace, his gravelly voice reflecting the seriousness of the situation. "They've called in the Ancients and I've been ordered to send you to Zeer. They believe the Eternians may be at the bottom of his disappearance."

"But, sir," Jessica responded to her chief, "the Eternians have been shut up in the crystal mines for over ten years now. How could they possibly be responsible?"

"All I know," Quad continued, "is that the Council wants the holofile on the Eternians re-opened to see if it might furnish a clue into Vantra's disappearance. I've given you

Federation clearance to access the file. Report back to me here at headquarters when you've seen it. End of transmission." Quad's image vanished from the screen.

Jessica returned to the lab. "Did you hear that Legend?"

"Yes," he replied. "I made a copy in case you might need it. You know, Jessica, I could run the Eternian holofile here if you like."

"That would mean accessing Federation computer banks."

"Yes...well, who's to know?" he answered slyly.

Jessica paused for a moment, pinching the bridge of her nose. "All right, bring up the file, let's see what we can find."

A myriad of multicolored lights blinked along the surface of Legend's screen as he downloaded the file. Scenes of the Eternian's defeat and arrest appeared in three dimensions. It was the first time Jessica had seen their plight and she was surprised at the effect it had on her. She was used to bringing hardened criminals, Evaders, to justice, not this mass hysteria associated with the roundup of human beings.

"Not pleasant, huh?"

Jessica had been so intent on the images she flinched at the sound of Legend's voice. "What did those people do to deserve that kind of treatment?" she asked, more to herself than Legend. "Didn't they realize they couldn't win against the Federation?"

"Evidently not," Legend replied.

The scene shifted to Prince Vantra, a look of triumph on his sardonic face, as he addressed the people of New Earth. His voice rose in volume to proclaim the imminent imprisonment of all Eternians, and their deportation to the abandoned crystal mines of Pragora on the planet Zeer.

"The pompous ass. I've never agreed with Vantra's demagog politics, and this is a classic example."

"You seem upset, Jessica."

"You know, Legend," she replied thoughtfully, "sitting here watching this holofile, it brought to mind a conversation I had had with father shortly before his death. Something regarding the Eternians."

Chin resting on fingertips, Jessica tried to recall the incident. Then lifting her head, she said, "Now I remember. Father inferred that the Eternians possessed something Prince Vantra feared. Maybe that's why he wanted them out of the way. From what we've seen here, I think he certainly accomplished his purpose."

"But, Jessica," Legend said, "the Eternians opposed the Prince. He *was* within his rights to break the uprising. Just because he asked the people of New Earth to abandon the old ways was no reason for the Eternians to rebel. Besides, as far as the old ways are concerned, people are no longer interested anyway."

"That's true, Legend, but—"

"It makes sense the Council would suspect the Eternians were responsible for Vantra's disappearance," Legend interrupted; proving he was not in the least intimidated by the fact he was a computer.

"Nonsense, Legend. Do you really believe the Eternians could manage such a feat right under the noses of Vantra's BorCron guards? Not to mention the fact that the Eternians have been sealed up in the caves for the past ten years. And speaking of Vantra's guards, where were they when this happened? Something doesn't fit."

"Your instincts are usually right, Jessica, but the Eternians do have every reason to want him out of the way. What if they *are* at the bottom of his disappearance?"

"All right," she replied. "Let's say purely for discussion's sake you're right. Where would they take him? Surely not to the caves, not with a squad of BorCrons patrolling the area.

According to Quad, the seals are still intact and there are no signs of anyone leaving the caves, or entering for that matter, and the sweeper pods are activated after each BorCron check."

"I don't know..." Legend spoke hesitantly.

"Neither do I," Jessica said mystified. "Maybe there's something we've missed?"

"Would you like to see the holofile again?" Legend asked.

All this intense focusing had given Jessica a headache. She hadn't eaten since early dawn and her stomach was objecting with rumblings she could no longer conceal. She glanced at Legend. *Sometimes I think he's more human than I am*, she thought with amusement.

As though reading her thoughts Legend said, "Sounds like you're ready for a break. With all that rumbling going on I thought we'd started our own battle."

"Wise guy." Jessica playfully rapped his console with the back of her hand.

"What do you say to a cool drink and some bread strips with moss cheese?" Legend asked. "We can chat while you eat."

"All right, I am hungry. But If I didn't know better, I'd think you just wanted company," she teased.

"Can I help it that your father gave me feelings along with this great brain?"

Legend's mention of her father sent Jessica's thoughts drifting back to that time of deep despair in her life.

She was eighteen when he had been killed in an explosion which had completely destroyed the lab he and his assistant, Weston Steiner, had been working in. The cause of the explosion was uncertain. At the time the two men had been involved in a project to stabilize the distortion of time created by wormholes in space. Her father's charred remains were found under a splintered beam. Ryden had been killed instantly, but Weston, badly burned, lay in the hospital in a coma struggling for life. Jessica had been at his bedside one evening, two days later, when for a brief moment he had regained consciousness. His eyes focused on her pale face and he spoke in a low croak. "Didn't...know...he...would..." Those had been the only words he had uttered. When Weston died the following day the judgment for his, and her father's death, had been officially labeled, "accidental."

I can't accept the fact that Father and Weston might have initiated something to cause that explosion. Father worked on dangerous experiments before and used the utmost caution. Why then, had that one been different? It seemed she would never be free of the nagging doubts that assailed her. If it hadn't been for Legend she didn't know how she would have gotten through those horrible days.

Legend understood her as no human could and it was to him she clung for comfort. Ever since her father had built him they were like family. She and Legend talked throughout the dark lonely hours of her pain. About how her father had raised her by himself when Jessica's mother died shortly after Jessica's fourth birthday. She had been too young to remember her mother, except for a vision of dark brown eyes crinkled in amusement. Her father used to say, "Your mother's eyes were so brown you could hardly see the pupils, and they always seemed to be smiling."

Jessica thought now of her father's dear voice. That precious gift he had bestowed to Legend. Her father's legacy; her family now.

Jessica shook her head, expunging the haunting memories. *It won't bring him back,* she thought sadly, *but at least I have that precious part of him.* She smiled at Legend and with a sigh willed herself to the work at hand.

* * *

Headache gone and hunger abated, Jessica instructed Legend to begin the Eternian holofile again. Leaning forward in her chair, she studied the lifelike scenes being played out before her, like a director observing the characters in a play.

She raised her hand. "Slow the imagery a bit, Legend."

Vantra's BorCron guards were roughly herding men, women, and children into a nearby hovertrain. In the distance, cries of, "monster, liar, deceiver," could be heard above the blasts of lasers and terrain disintegrators.

Jessica pointed. "There. Stop there."

Her attention was drawn to a stooped elderly-looking man with silver hair being jostled and pushed into the train along with several others.

"He appears feeble enough." Her voice was hesitant. "I wonder...Enhance the image."

Legend homed in as directed while Jessica pinned her attention on the man's bent form. His head was turned away from her and she couldn't make out his features, but his hands were smooth with no sign of aging as his posture implied. His dark clothing blended with the train's interior, as did the object partially hidden in the crook of one arm.

"He's holding something, Legend, can you bring it into focus?"

Legend drew in intently on the object in question. "From what I can see, Jessica, it looks like a large book, but that's all I can make out. It's partially concealed by his coat."

"Hmmm...Why a book?" she mused aloud. "You'd think the BorCron guard next to him would have picked it up with his sensoring device?"

"From the way the BorCron is ignoring him I'd say he's not even aware of the man," commented Legend. "It would seem this one possesses the ability to block the BorCron's sensor."

"But the only ones who could do that were..."

"Androids," finished Legend.

Jessica frowned. "But all New Earth Androids were wiped out over twelve years ago when the Trobieen Virus invaded their synthetic organs. How is it one could have survived?"

"We don't know for sure, Jessica, if he *is* an Android, but if so, chances are he could have been on another planet at the time."

"That is a possibility," she said thoughtfully. "But the Federation strictly forbade the transporting of Androids because of the virus. I'll have to report this development to the Council. If he's aligned himself with the Eternians he could pose a threat."

"Do you think he might be involved with Vantra's disappearance?"

"I don't know..." Jessica replied hesitantly. "But I have to wonder, however, what connection he might have with the Eternians? It's possible he could have been acting on his own and gotten swept up with them, but one thing's for certain, he was taken to the caves along with the others. I think it might be wise to inform Quad before I report to the Council. I don't want to stir up more trouble than I have to. From what I've seen, those people have had enough of that already. I know it's a matter of doing my job and leaving the Council to deal with the legal aspects, but sometimes I can't help wondering..." Her voice trailed off as though she were reluctant to express aloud her remaining thoughts.

Legend's voice softened as he reminded her, "Your father told me how proud he was of you when you received your badge and uniform. I know if he were here today he'd tell you to do what you feel is right."

"It's not as though I have an option," replied Jessica. "As a Chaser I'm sworn to uphold Federation law. But there's nothing that says I have to like it," she added.

"Of course, there's always *appeal*," replied Legend.

"Appeal would release me from the assignment, but…no, I'll do what must be done and hope for the best. Besides, these Eternians interest me; I wonder what they're like."

Chapter 2
The Council of Six

Jessica punched in Quad's number on her visual and informed him of her suspicions concerning the Android.

"You'd better prepare yourself for the Council," Quad remarked. "They've called me to see where you are on the case. I informed them you would be there within the hour to make your report. And, Jessica."

"Yes, sir?"

"Good work. I know they've chosen the right person."

"Thank you, sir." She blinked off the visual and hurried into the bedroom to change into her dress uniform.

An hour later, standing at stiff attention, Jessica waited before the elevated dais upon which Vantra's Council of Six sat behind a curved marble table; their robes of deep bronze displayed in stark contrast against the whiteness of the marble. Mantles of authority draped each shoulder in graceful folds, held in place by braided straps overlaid in silver. Beneath the bronze and silver cap of each man, thick hair flowed past the neck and lay in white profusion along his back; perfect clones of Prince Vantra.

Three steps above the dais of the Council rested the Seat of Knowledge overlooking the Hall where Vantra held court and where Jessica now stood. To her left was a visual screen and hologram platform. Two large statues guarded the otherwise barren room; each draped in the familiar mantel of authority, resembling the six men before her.

Like a marble tomb, she thought. Her eyes moved farther up to where the sphere of the Ancients floated above the heads of the Council. Eons ago they had abandoned their human form, their essence now dwelling in this mystical sphere, seemingly aloof and indifferent, until called upon to assist the Council in important matters of state. Where the Ancients came from, or what they did when they were not advising Vantra's court, was a mystery. When Kordon Faus had been Prefect, he sought their valued advice, but Prince Vantra gave the impression he could manage New Earth very well without them. Now he was gone, disappeared without a trace. In his absence the Council thought it wise to at least give the impression they were seeking the Ancients help.

One of the men broke the silence. "Chaser Caldar, Chief Quad has informed us you uncovered the possibility of an Android in connection with the Eternians. How did you come by this information?"

"Are you sure what you saw was an Android?" questioned another man.

"And what is this about a book?" inquired yet a third.

Omitting Legend's involvement, she began respectfully, "Your Excellencies. As you requested I researched the holofile on the Eternians from the Federation's computer banks, which I have downloaded into your computer. Upon close examination I uncovered the details I now show you."

At her command light emanated from beneath the dais and three-dimensional images flashed into motion. Jessica instructed the computer to project the desired scene and drew the Council's attention to the hunched man in black, pointing out the seemingly inability of the BorCron to detect either the man or his book.

"As your Excellencies know, Androids possessed Bio-Waves designed especially to disrupt sensors enabling them to infiltrate enemy territory undetected. When the Trobieen Virus destroyed all of New Earth's Androids, Prince Vantra had his BorCron guards equipped with this same ability. If this is an Android, and I'm sure it is, there's no way the guards would have been able to detect him."

The Council watched with interest, whispering occasionally one to another. When they had seen enough they signaled her to cease. Jessica voiced a command and the images dissolved. The Council nodded in unison then one of the men spoke.

"You were right to bring this to our attention. As Chief Quad's best Chaser, this Council is in agreement that you should be the one to travel to planet Zeer and investigate the crystal mines of Pragora. If this Android is still in service your orders are to destroy it by whatever means."

Jessica couldn't help wondering why the Android needed to be destroyed but thought better of questioning the Council. *At least not until I've gotten some answers of my own,* she thought.

"Should you find a connection between these dissenters and Prince Vantra's disappearance you will contact us immediately. Is that understood?"

"Quite, Your Excellencies," Jessica replied stiffly.

"You are dismissed."

With that, she turned smartly and retreated from the hall.

Chapter 3
Quad

Having changed from her braided dress uniform into gray regulars, Jessica waited at the entrance to Central Command while the computer scanned her palm for identification.

"Palm identification confirmed," the feminine voice intoned. "Please move forward for retina scanning."

Jessica rested her forehead against the scanner's smooth surface as two red beams crisscrossed over her eyes.

"Retina identification confirmed. You may enter, Chaser Caldar."

As the sealed door whooshed open a wall of sound greeted her reverberating from every direction as she stepped through to the command center. Control terminals hummed and flashed their signals like a dense city awakening from a solar eclipse. Against concave walls above the consoles, monitors blinked in a profusion of color as information spilled across their screens. Shadows curled and wafted along the ceiling reflecting the movements of those below, and in the midst of this orderly confusion, she heard her name bellowed.

"Caldar...! It's about time you got here!"

The strident voice of Quad rang in her ears. She chuckled inwardly. *I'd recognize that voice in the middle of a blaster tunnel with everyone firing at once.* Jessica skirted around the busy room and strode up to face the, not-so-smiling, impressive figure of her chief. The square jawed Borkian stood with arms crossed and black eyes fixed on her approach.

Quad came from the planet Borkia in the Eastern Quadrant of Dadessery. Its two surrounding atmospheres reverberating against each another created an echo chamber, and Quad, like his ancestors, retained the ability to open and close his ear channels at will allowing sound levels to suit himself. With the exception of lidless eyes, and four fingered hands he resembled most Earthmen.

He had been sent to Bostonia twenty-five years earlier as a Chaser. He learned the language and worked his way through the ranks to chief. Under his command Jessica had blossomed into a prime Chaser. Some of the others felt she was soft, but Quad knew she possessed a quality of strength even she was unaware of.

He recalled the day she had entered the academy. Standing at stiff attention under his most disconcerting scrutiny, her startling green eyes never wavered. Even his six-foot-five frame towering over her, pupils narrowed into black menacing slits, hadn't made her blanch. Of course Jessica had no way of knowing this was Quad's usual way of testing raw recruits, weeding out those who might knuckle under in a crisis. The faintest curve had tweaked the edges of her lips. He soon sensed this auburn-haired beauty wasn't the least bit afraid of him, no matter how intimidating he looked. Nor was there a fear scent surrounding her like so many others he had put to the test. This was another of his ancestral traits, the ability to smell fear, like smoke boiling up from a wet log. He was a good judge of character and Jessica Caldar possessed a quality yet to be tested.

***

"Step into my office, Jessica, since you don't have ears like mine I'm sure you'll hear better out of this din." He held the door open and waited for her to step inside, then motioned her to a chair as he moved to sit behind his desk. A picture of his wife and two small sons stood in a wooden frame to Jessica's left. She picked up the picture. At her touch the figures within the frame became animated, as when the vid-photo had been taken. Augueen was smiling affectionately at her two sons, Condee and Retsel, as the two boys proudly displayed their new pet mocker, Poom, its cat-like form held up to the vid-camera by the younger of the two boys.

"Say hello, Poom," Retsel urged in Earth language.

"Say hello," Poom repeated, mocking Retsel's voice. The two boys giggled.

Augueen smiled ruefully into the vid-camera. "We miss you." Then the figures stood immobile once again within the frame.

"When do you expect them back?" Jessica asked, replacing the picture.

"Augueen says it will be two more Earth days before she and the boys can leave Borkia. Her mother is well over a hundred now and Augueen wanted to spend as much time with her as possible. Borkia will be drifting out of Zeer's orbit soon so they'll have to catch the next shuttle to Pragora."

Jessica had become acquainted with Quad's wife during many of the official gatherings she had attended. Augueen was just the opposite of her stiff official husband. Her sense of humor was a delight, and she was quite beautiful. For some reason Augueen had taken a liking to Jessica, always making sure she was invited to their parties.

"If things work out, sir, maybe I'll be in Pragora about the same time. I hope I'll be able to see her."

"It's quite possible," Quad replied. "I know Augueen would enjoy seeing you again." He moved from behind the desk and settled himself on one of its edges, his arm resting on a knee. "The Council wants you to leave right away. They're worried that the longer Prince Vantra is gone, the weaker their power. I think they're afraid of the Ancients."

Quad shifted his large frame from the desk to the chair opposite Jessica. "I'm reasonably sure the Eternians had nothing to do with Vantra's disappearance, but if anyone can get to the bottom of this I know you can, Jessica."

"I appreciate your confidence in me, Chief, but after what Prince Vantra did to them I hardly think they're likely to tell me anything. Chasers were involved in their capture ten years ago and I doubt if there's any love lost, even if we're trying to help."

"Let's not jump to conclusions just yet," Quad stated. "If they are innocent we need to find proof."

Jessica shifted in her chair her eyes met his. "Sir, you seem to be more interested in proving their innocence than their guilt. Is there something you're not telling me?"

Quad looked hard at Jessica as though he were debating something in his mind. Then having come to a decision answered. "Since you're a part of this now I think you should know I was involved in the imprisonment and transporting of the Eternians to the mines."

Jessica stared at him, but didn't speak, waiting for him to continue.

"I was working my way up to chief and didn't dare disobey a direct order. Being a Borkian made it that much harder." Quad lifted his sturdy frame from the chair and stood for a moment with his back to her, then turned and continued. "Borkia built an empire worthy of New Earth's own, but it wasn't until the last century we began sending ambassadors across the galaxy. I came as a young recruit to learn about New Earth's system of Chasers and stayed. I worked hard for my promotions and, to tell the truth, Jessica, didn't care whose toes I stepped on to get there. I was up for chief when this thing with the Eternians erupted. I knew my job was at stake if I didn't follow through with Prince Vantra's orders, but working alongside his BorCron guards gave me a new perspective. Their cruelty towards their prisoners went beyond reason and I began to suspect Vantra had more than rebellion against them. I figured the only way I could help the Eternians was to work within the system, but I've been unable to do anything until now. The Council's orders have given me what I need to speak to them and discover why they were singled out."

Jessica stood, frowning. "Just what is it you think I can do, sir? I appreciate the fact you have sympathy for these people, I tend to myself, but I'm under official orders to find Prince Vantra. That's my sole purpose, and if it turns out they *are* responsible I have to report that to the Council."

"No, I want you to report directly to me."

Jessica looked surprised.

Quad continued. "I'm not asking you to deviate from your directive. I *want* you to find Prince Vantra and question the Eternians. All I'm asking is that you report to me before reporting to the Council." He waited for her answer.

She knew in effect he was accepting responsibility should there be an accounting.

"Very well, Chief, I understand." Resuming her seat, she offered what information she had. "According to the surveillance that's been in force these past ten years the Eternians are rarely seen. If it weren't for the space generators left by the miners after the Pragorian crystal was no longer needed for trade, they never would have survived this long."

Quad settled back into his desk chair and folded his hands. "The Ancients advised the Council against destroying the equipment. It turned out to be a good thing for the Eternians."

"I can't help wondering," Jessica said, "why the Ancients should care about what happens to them."

"Yes...it's always puzzled me too..." he said, leaning forward and resting his arms on the desk. "I'm hoping you'll find answers to these questions when you talk to the Eternians, but right now let's get to the work at hand. I've made arrangements for you on the spaceship, Glennden. She leaves tomorrow night and will dock at Space Station Oron. From there you'll transport down to the Pragorian command post. I've sent word ahead to one of our Chasers, Jarod Krinner. He'll see to it that you have everything you'll need for your stay, and also escort you into the caves." Quad tilted back his chair in dismissal. "Good luck."

Chapter 4
Protandel

Protandel tensed and pressed deeper into the shadows as Jessica exited the command center and moved in the opposite direction towards New State Avenue, unaware she was being followed. His orders were to report her movements. What they didn't know was that he had no intention of delivering Caldar into their hands. He had his own agenda. The contact inside Chaser Headquarters had informed him she was to leave for Zeer on the Glennden within twelve hours. He would have to strike soon, he thought, before she boarded. In the meantime he would bide his time keeping her in sight. Savoring what was to come, he slipped from the shadows and stealthily followed.

***

Quad began pacing restlessly as soon as Jessica left his office, his thoughts on their conversation. His long strides propelled him from one end of the room to the other then back again.

Why had the Council waited two days before reporting Vantra's disappearance?

Quad's eyes narrowed into black slits as he recalled how he had been called before The Council of Six ten years ago and ordered to assist Prince Vantra's elite guard in rounding up the Eternians for shipment to Pragora. He had seen then how the BorCrons worked. Their methods went beyond Federation law, but then Vantra considered himself the law.

The Eternians were never a threat to Vantra, he thought. *Vantra's the one who stirred things up by forcing his so-called "Enlightenment" on them. As far as I can see, the only enlightenment he's brought to New Earth is a kind of mind control. There's more to this than meets the eye.*

A rapid knock on his office door jolted Quad from his angry thoughts.

"Yes, what is it!" he snapped, flinging open the door. The surprised cadet who stood on the threshold stepped back in alarm as if he thought Quad meant to strike him.

Quad spoke, less threatening. "What is it, Thatcher?"

"Sir, you have an incoming dispatch. Shall I relay it to you here?"

Quad ran a hand over the back of his neck. "Yes. Sorry about that, Thatcher, didn't mean to explode on you."

Thatcher nodded and exited Quad's office. "Wow, what was that all about?"

Chapter 5
Old Capital

As Jessica departed the busy turmoil of headquarters, warm sunshine bathed her, dispelling her gray thoughts, like a swift breeze through dense fog.

A stroll to Old Capital Museum might be just the thing to clear my head before returning to my quarters, she thought. A breath of air from one of the temperature control vents wafted across her face lightly lifting a tress of her auburn hair. Brushing the wayward strand aside she raised her face to the overhead sun shield. *Zeer will be cold this time of year, not to mention Pragora and the caves.* Despite the warm rays of artificial sun an unexplained shiver strummed its way along her spine.

The museum was only a mile from headquarters and although the moving walkway overhead would get her to her destination sooner, she chose to walk. As always there were an abundance of airjet cars, trams and cabs silently skimming along computer charted airways to their various destinations. She passed shops uniquely decorated in splashes of brilliant color to attract the many tourists flocking to the city. The smells of exotic foods drifted on the air as fellow pedestrians bustled along, working their way up and down New State Avenue. Bostonia was a large city filled with exciting things to see, but today she was in the mood to view relics of a past civilization, long vanished but not entirely forgotten. Although she had visited Old Capital many times, its history, like an old friend, was something she never tired of.

Arriving in time to board the tourist airtram, she slid her Interplanetary Transaction card through the narrow slot at the computer station and settled into an empty seat. A stout woman slid into the place next to her and smiled. Several couples moved into adjoining seats and were quietly talking to one another or fellow passengers. A short muscular man boarded and moved down the aisle. As he passed, Jessica caught a brief glimpse of his sallow, pitted face. For a moment she thought she recognized him and turned to get a closer look. But he was already seated out of her line of vision. She shrugged and turned her attention to the view as the airtram began its smooth assent over the ancient ruins.

"Old Capital is known to have been the oldest city in Early Earth's history," the onboard computer droned. "According to the Society of Ancient Times, Old Capital was once the political center of a vast nation known as, the United States of America. Asteroid swarms of tremendous proportion struck Earth in the year 2225 destroying the capital, along with hundreds of cities. Devastation to the ozone caused polar caps to melt, creating floods around the world. Eventually, the sun scorched Earth left rivers and lakes decimated and oceans empty of life. Earth had become a sterile planet, desolate and barren."

Though Jessica had heard this many times, still it held a fascination for her.

The computer continued. "Survivors of this great

catastrophe migrated to other planets throughout the galaxy. Earth was left to dust and decay until the year 2340 when colonists returned to begin reconstruction under the Federation of Planets. Many brought with them maps, documents and pictures of Earth preserved by earlier ancestors, enabling the society to locate and restore a greater part of Old Capital. However, after three hundred years, still most of Earth remains as you see it here."

Jessica recalled pictures of Early Earth she had seen in the Archives of Ancient History. Green forests stretching beyond the human eye, flowing rivers cascading over magnificent waterfalls, and flowers, so brilliant of color even the glass frames that encased them failed to fade their delicate beauty. There were replicas of several different species of animals as well, but their empty staring eyes seemed a mockery of the living, breathing animals they portrayed.

How beautiful Earth must have been, she thought. *Not as it is now; colonies built beneath domed spheres, maintained by giant computers within their core to escape atmospheric poisons; and beyond, only desolation. Even food, water and air produced by artificial means.*

Jessica sighed as she gazed at craters pock-marking the surface below. Black mud caked their interiors; large boulders lay scattered around their crusted rims, appearing as though they might topple in at any moment, but petrified and frozen in time.

Perhaps somewhere in the solar system there's another Earth waiting to be explored, she thought.

The tram drifted along its pre-assigned path to three other sites described as memorials to several great men of America.

"An even greater discovery," continued the computer as they descended to an enormous excavation site, "is this building found buried beneath tons of debris. It is what the

Early Earth people called their Capitol. Archaeologists uncovered within its depths an enormous library containing massive amounts of books, pictures, drawings, and maps of America, as well as thousands of official documents stored in ancient vaults. These, as well as the documents brought back by the early colonists, provided excellent details of Early Earth's government three hundred years ago."

Yes, Jessica thought, *and when Vantra came into power he removed some of those documents from the Society of Ancient Times, under the pretext of handing them over to the Federation, but they were never received.* Was it possible, she wondered, that those particular documents could have influenced the Federation, creating a shift in Vantra's controlling power?

Sometime later, having circled several new excavations in progress, the tour came to an end. Jessica exited the tram just as the last rays of the setting sun glowed red across the artificial horizon, highlighting fiery flecks of gold through her hair.

Chapter 6
Jarod

Jarod Krinner lay stretched across his bunk fighting insomnia. He willed his body to relax and accept sleep, but it was no use. With a sigh of resignation, he tossed back the covers and swung his bare feet to the floor. Sitting, with bent elbows on knees, he brushed strong fingers through his already disheveled hair.

Striking in appearance, his tall frame and broad shoulders lent strength to his handsomely chiseled features. His gray, deep-set eyes often held an intensity that seemed to see right through people. Thick black hair fell in waves to the nape of his neck, at times unruly, causing him to run his fingers through it impatiently, as he was now doing.

He thought about his assignment with Jessica Caldar. *Wonder what she's like. According to the files on Apprehended Evaders, her effectiveness as a Chaser was quite impressive. Must be a bit of a tough bird.*

Rising from his bunk he dressed and headed for the Operations Room.

Might as well make some use of this night.

Chapter 7
Naal and Protandel

Jessica checked her watch. Just past six. Spotting a nearby hailport she decided to take a cab back to her living quarters. As she moved towards the hailport, Protandel ducked into the nearest doorway. He knew if she saw him she would recognize him as the man on the airtram and become suspicious. Face averted, he kept to the shadows and pretended to browse over the wrist computers displayed in one of the shop windows. After a few moments he chanced a look in her direction just in time to see her enter a cab and settle herself inside. He had a good idea where she was headed, and since he knew where she lived he didn't feel rushed to follow. Opening his jacket, he extracted a palm visual from an inside pocket and tapped in the coded number.

"I'm continuing my surveillance. Departure is as planned. Caldar is due to transport down as expected. I've transmitted the coordinates to our informant aboard the Glennden. Any instructions?"

Naal's scowl filled the small screen. "No, but if she misses that transfer beam we might as well blast ourselves into a sun flare. It will be quicker than what will happen if we fail."

If I fail it won't matter, Protandel thought, pocketing the visual.

***

Naal was a giant of a man in his fifties, muscular and hairy with deep lines etched into his broad dark face. He wore his long beard in two braids tucked beneath his extended jaw. Like his entire race, his nostrils consisted of two wide slits above large lips. His ears, sunken into a wide skull, rode high on his temples. He and his new partner, Protandel, were mercenary warriors who sold their services to the highest bidder.

They had crossed paths on G. Sector of Acronon-Five, a small rogue planet that had the reputation of harboring Evaders and Mercenaries. Not many ships ventured into her path; those that did were usually slave traders, or had contraband to sell. Even though Protandel was an Earthling, Naal had taken a liking to the man. Over a few drinks and cautious conversation, Naal learned Protandel had served time in prison.

"I killed a man on New Earth," he told Naal. "A Federation Chaser caught up with me at my brother's before I could clear out. My brother was killed trying to protect me and I was shipped to prison. I managed to escape after serving five years and came here, but not before I learned the Chaser's name and where she lives." Protandel gulped the remainder of his drink and slammed the container down hard on the bar.

"Jessica Caldar will regret the day our paths ever crossed, she'll pay with her life for my brother's death and the years I spent rotting in that hellhole!"

Naal was about to disclose to Protandel an assignment

given to him involving the very person they had been discussing when a scarred face Tropin brushed past him causing Naal to spill his drink. Naal calmly picked the man up with one hand, set him on the bar, and smashed a bottle of Soono over his head. The green liquid splattered over the Tropin's head, down his limp body and pooled on the bar. Two Jings standing at the bar extended their long serpentine tongues and lapped up the spilled fluid then went on with their conversation.

"Damn Tropins, I hate 'em!" Naal growled. "They smell like hell. Most of their slaves don't even make it this far. They have pets called Uggers that can eat a whole man in less than a nura. They're used to clean up the carnage." Naal opened his hand and let the Tropin topple forward from the bar face down onto the spittle laden floor.

"Now where was I," he continued, as though this were a common occurrence in his mercenary life. "Yeah, I think, Protandel, I have a job you might be interested in."

***

Protandel waited until Jessica's cab was out of sight before calling up one of his own. He punched in his purchase code instructing the computer, then sat back in anticipation as the control panel displayed a map of his destination.

I wonder what Naal and the others will do when they find out I'm not their messenger boy. They can go to hell, Caldar's mine. A cold smile steeled across his lips as he contemplated his long overdue revenge.

Arriving at Jessica's quarters Protandel waited, allowing her time to get inside before he alighted and pressed the "Unoccupied" button on the cab's side panel, sending it on its way. He skirted the edge of the high wall surrounding her property and resumed his vigil within its shadowed depths.

Chapter 8
Intruder

Jessica's voice key opened the door. As she stepped through the entrance a series of lights threaded their way around the room.

She had made few changes to the dwelling she and her father had shared before his death. A high wall separated the living quarters from other buildings in the area, giving her ample privacy. On the outside it appeared much the same as other structures in that location, with one exception; a secret lab lay hidden within the hollow of one of its exterior walls. Virtual bubble ceilings obscured the interior from overhead traffic, at the same time allowing in ample light during the day, and star laden skies at night.

Jessica's taste did not lean towards elaborate furnishings, however the living space was quite pleasant. A feminine touch was evident in the soft accenting colors throughout, but on the whole, the furniture was simple and functional. Four rooms faced inward to a central garden, profuse with plants and brilliantly colored flowers. Sparkles of blue water cascaded into a pond filled with exotic fish swimming in quiet splendor; all a fabrication of the real thing. Scenes of Early Earth's beauty were projected by hologram around the circular walls.

Skirting the pool she entered her bedroom and instructed Legend to relay any messages.

"Welcome home, Jessica. No messages received," he responded.

Leaving her uniform and boots scattered across the carpet, Jessica stepped into the micro-shower. Later, wearing a robe of green velvet that matched her eyes, she sat comfortably in a lounge chair by the pond eating a light meal and sipping wine. Her thoughts turned briefly to her contact, Jarod Krinner. *I hope he's not some know-it-all who thinks I can't handle the situation.*

Stretching, and stifling a yawn, Jessica rose from her chair and moved toward the far wall. It appeared she might smash into it if she continued her course. Instead, the illusion wall wavered and split like a shimmering waterfall and she passed through into the secret lab her father had built to house Legend.

Ryden Caldar had programmed the gateway to identify only his and Jessica's DNA, although it could be activated from inside by Legend. Jessica recalled the first time she had stepped through the gateway as a child and proclaimed, "It tickles, Daddy." He had laughed and swung her up into his arms.

"Promise me, my sweet girl, you will never tell anyone about Legend or this lab. It will be our secret. Mine, yours and Legend's."

"I promise, Daddy, don't worry, I won't tell a soul."

She was only seven at the time but knew the importance of what her father was asking of her and she would keep that promise.

Legend had become not only her mentor after her father's death, but her friend and confidant. It was to him she turned to pour out her sorrow, and to him she endowed her trust.

***

"How long do you plan to be on Zeer?" Legend inquired.

"That will depend on the cooperation we get from the Eternians," Jessica replied.

"We?"

"Yes. Quad informed me at the last minute that I'm to be met by someone from the Pragorian colony. Really, Legend, I've been a Chaser for eight years now and brought in my share of Evaders, you'd think Quad could trust me to go this alone."

"I don't think trust is the question, Jessica, he knows what he's doing. But right now we need to set your brain wave communicator so I can keep in touch with you telepathically."

Jessica opened a small drawer attached to Legend's console and extracted a small device resembling a worm. As she pressed the communicator to her ear it seemed to take on a life of its own and wriggled forward to disappear within its depths.

"Set your voice module to its lowest level and give me a test run," she said.

After speaking several words in a soft, almost inaudible whisper, he asked, "How's that?"

"Fine. Now set for inner voice."

Legend adjusted the device to her brainwave, enabling them to communicate telepathically. "Contact me when you get to the caves," he said. "And for now I suggest you get some sleep."

Jessica removed the communicator from her ear and slipped it into her robe pocket. "Yes, I am tired," she said, stifling a yawn with the back of her hand. "Are the perimeter sensors activated?"

"Done."

"Good night, Legend."

"Good night, Jessica. Sleep well."

He opened the gateway and she stepped through moving into her bedroom. Shedding the velvet robe, she tossed it over a chair and slid beneath the soft covers of her bed and was soon asleep.

Cold tendrils of fog drifted up from the damp ground soaking her gown in black mud. She was in a tunnel, surrounded by walls of dirt and debris. She tried to call out but her voice was frozen within her throat. Ahead lay a murky curtain of darkness, and behind, a void that threatened to engulf her. A man's voice pierced the gloom calling her name, but she was unable to answer. She waited, listening, dreading the silence, her heart beating a tableau of fear. I'm here, she cried mutely. His form took shape cleaving the misty fog. Arms outstretched he beckoned to enfold her. His features were blurred, but somehow she knew she would be safe within those arms, if only...

"Jessica...wake up, we have an intruder," Legend's voice ripped through her dream. She awoke with a start, her training bringing her to full alert.

"Location?" she asked, as she quickly dressed and reentered the lab.

"Inside the wall at the northern perimeter."

"All right," Jessica said in a low voice, "whoever you are, let's see what you have in mind. Can you tell if it's male or female?"

"Male."

"Bring him on screen and let's take a look. He must have used a sensor disrupter to have gotten this far."

Legend focused on the crouched figure. The man hesitated for a moment, as though listening then moved in the direction of the back wall.

"He's heading towards the ventilation shaft," Legend said. "Probably hoping to gain entrance that way?"

"Yes, I think you're right. Let's see if we can change his mind. Close off the shaft. I'm going outside."

"Be careful, Jessica, we don't know what weapons he might be carrying."

"Keep tracking him on your monitor, Legend. If he manages to give me the slip I might still be able to identify him through Evader files. But right now I want to know what he's doing here."

Jessica armed herself and instructed Legend to extinguish all lights. She moved stealthily out into the moonlit surroundings. Her lithe movements brought her within twelve feet of the kneeling man whose back was toward her. He had shed his jacket as he worked prying open the cover to the ventilation shaft with a steel bar. His breathing was labored, muffling her approach as she crouched and moved closer, weapon raised. She was within five feet when her boot scraped against something hard. The man stiffened, jumped to his feet and whirled around, at the same time hurling the steel bar. Dodging aside, Jessica fired, but the momentum of her body sent the laser off target. Before she could fire again the intruder's body plummeted into her stunning her and knocking her backwards to the ground. The weapon spun from her grasp.

Protandel straddled her, encircling her throat with his rough hands. His dark, angry eyes, vivid in the moon's reflected light, glared down into her own. "How nice of you to save me the trouble of coming to you, Caldar. I've waited five years for this." His voice shook with emotion as his grip tightened.

Jessica felt the blood pulsate through her skull as air was sucked from her lungs. Her arms flailed out from her sides groping the ground, desperately trying to find a hold before she passed out. Her fingers came in contact with the metal bar. She grasped the cold steel rod and swung. Protandel's body jerked backwards loosening his grip from around her throat. He slumped to one side, stunned. Jessica rolled out from under him onto her knees her body racked with coughing. Too dazed to stand, hands pressed to the ground to support her weight, she gasped for breath, fighting to steady herself. But he came at her again before she had time to react. Lifting her upright off the ground by her lapels, he slammed her shoulders against the wall. Her head hit the hard surface with a thud sending sharp waves of dizziness through her brain. She felt as though every stone in the wall had been etched into her skull. The hands that pinned her were like steel and her efforts to break free were useless.

"Now, Caldar, let's see how well you die. Not as fast as my brother, I'll make sure of that, but just as dead."

Jessica was looking into the pockmarked face of the man on the hovertram, the man she now recognized as the Evader she had sent to prison five years earlier. Stalling for time until she could gather her strength, she asked through wheezing breath, "And just what have I got to do with your brother?"

His eyes blazed into hers. "Don't act the innocent with me, Caldar; I saw the recognition in your eyes. You know exactly who I am, the man who's going to end your life. You'll beg me to finish you off before I'm done. They thought I'd play their little game and act as their errand boy, but I've wanted you dead too long; *they* can go to hell!"

Before she could ask who *they* were, he spun her around hard, jamming her cheek into the pitted wall. Pain surged along her spine as he ground a knee into her back, at the same time forcing her chin upward with his left arm. With his free hand he slid a knife from his boot and rested it against her throat. As though having second thoughts, he moved the knife upward to her temple. "But first let's rearrange this pretty face."

Jessica struggled to twist away but a sharp nick of the blade caused her to cry out. A warm trickle of blood flowed from her hairline.

"This is just the beginning," he whispered into her ear, his arm like a vice, forcing her chin even higher. His breath was hot and foul against her face and she cringed when he slowly licked the blood from her cheek. "I'm disappointed, Caldar, I thought maybe you were something special, but you bleed like any human." His voice was full of disgust. "Let's see, I think a nice slit here." As his knife hand started its downward descent Jessica seized her opportunity. She whipped her head sideways and sank her teeth deep into his bare arm. Protandel let out a howl and the knife dropped from his fingers. Freed from his grasp she whirled around, catching him full in the stomach with her elbow. Strings of profanity escaped between his clenched teeth. He made a dive to retrieve the knife, but Jessica kicked it away. As he stumbled to his feet, she locked her hands and knocked him into the wall. Blood spurted from his mouth soaking the front of his shirt.

"I'm glad to see you bleed like any human," Jessica mocked, throwing his words back at him.

"You bitch, I'll kill you!" Protandel sprang away from the wall in a murderous rage, his anger making him careless.

"I think you've already tried that," she sneered.

He made a grab for her, but Jessica brought up her knee and caught him full in the groin doubling him over in pain. Picking up the steel bar, she slammed it hard across his exposed neck and Protandel folded in on himself dropping to the ground with a thud.

Jessica stood with legs apart, her breath coming in short spurts as she ran the back of her hand across her mouth, wiping away the metallic taste of her own blood. "I don't think I'll be seeing you again anytime soon," she said, staring down at the unconscious man. Opening her vid-com she contacted headquarters. "This is Chaser Caldar, send a couple of men to my quarters to pick up an Evader. Oh, and bring along a Med-Pack," she added.

Chapter 9
Deception

Prince Vantra paced the floor where he remained secretly in hiding, his thoughts on Jessica Caldar. *I'll ring the truth from her, but I must go carefully. Ryden was a fool, weak and old, but his daughter is young; young and strong.* A cruel smile spread across his lips.

Ceasing his pacing, Vantra turned to the mercenary, Naal. "Are you sure Protandel is tracking Caldar? I've gone to a lot of trouble to get her where I want her and I don't need idiots fouling it up!"

Naal stiffened at the word *"idiots,"* but managed to hold his temper in check. He watched with hooded eyes the man before him. He knew from experience, having been hired by Vantra more than once to do his dirty work, that the man was vicious and would stop at nothing to get what he wanted.

Vantra had informed Naal it was his intention to see that the Eternians would be blamed for his *alleged* disappearance, and Caldar sent to Pragora to investigate. How Vantra managed to accomplish all this Naal had no idea, nor did he care. He was well paid for his services and not about to jeopardize things by asking questions.

He wondered how this earthling managed to gain such power over the Galactic Federation. Granted the man had a charisma that moved people to follow him, but few saw beyond his ability to lead, into the man himself. *If insanity makes a leader,* Naal mused, *Vantra certainly fits the bill.*

"Vantra—" Naal started to speak, but before he could finish Vantra raged at him.

"You address me by my proper title or by damn I'll have your hairy hide flayed off your back! Do I make myself clear?"

Naal blanched, but kept his voice level as he replied. "Quite clear, Your Highness."

Vantra's voice was low and menacing. "You were about to say?"

Naal felt the bile rise to the back of his throat. His gut twisted in anger, but he managed to keep his voice even as he answered. "I was saying, *Your Highness,* that Protandel has secured the coordinates Caldar will use to transport down to Pragora from the space platform."

"Excellent," Vantra replied, a look of smugness on his face. "In a few hours Jessica Caldar will be wondering what went wrong, and I'll be only too happy to fill in the blanks."

Naal's cold stare followed Vantra as he swiftly turned and stalked from the room, white hair and bronze robe flowing out behind him like an ancient bird of prey.

Chapter 10
Aboard the Glennden

The Federation ship, Glennden, rested at its docking port as the crew made ready to depart. She was one of the finest cruisers in the fleet, used specifically for transporting Prince Vantra and planetary diplomats. Equipped with folded space drive, she could out-run anything in the galaxy that posed a threat. However, most of her inner structure was given over to the comfort of her passengers. The Glennden's orders were to receive the Urian ambassador aboard from Pragora, and transport Jessica down from the space-docking platform.

Jessica arrived at the port in time for departure. Stiff and bruised from her ordeal with Protandel, still she managed a sheepish grin when the young ensign who greeted her asked with concern, "Are you all right?"

"I ran into a brick wall," Jessica replied to her question, touching the bandaged cut at her temple, "one with hands."

"Do I dare ask who won?" the young woman asked with amusement.

"Let's just say there's one less Evader to worry about," Jessica chuckled.

"It's good you can still joke about it," the woman said with a smile. She turned and motioned Jessica to follow her down a plush carpeted hatchway.

"Here we are," she said, pausing before a steel door. "I hope you'll be comfortable. We've been told you are to have the run of the ship. I'd be happy to escort you around if you'd like?"

"I appreciate the offer, but that won't be necessary. What is our arrival time at the space platform?"

"We should dock within the next eighteen hours. Is there anything I can get you?"

"No, I'm fine thank you."

"Well, if you should think of anything there are voice activated monitors in every room." She smiled at Jessica then turned and moved back along the hatchway.

Several chambers lined the corridor on either side. Jessica assumed they were for visiting dignitaries. Entering what she imagined would be simple sleeping quarters, she paused on the threshold. *There must be some mistake*, she thought, as motion activated lights illuminated an opulent white-carpeted lounge decorated with ebony lamps and white sofas. Murals, of iridescent colors framed the room.

Three lights blinked like gleaming stones on the pedestal to her right. She passed her hand over the one marked Viewer Port. Shimmering drapes of metallic silver slid open with a gentle burr…revealing a porthole the width of one wall. She moved to the window and stood for several moments gazing intently at the star laden sky before her. *So quiet and peaceful*, she thought. *As though time and space have given way to something eternal.*

Sighing, she turned from the tranquil scene and continued her inspection. In the center of the bedroom stood a large bed encircled in a cocoon of sheer veils. *Almost too pretty to sleep on,* she thought, sweeping aside one of the veils and running her palms over the bed's silky surface.

Removing her uniform jacket, she draped it over a nearby chair, then the belt encircling her waist. She slid off her side pack and weapon, leaving the transmitter attached, then refastened the belt. Tossing her cap aside, she began unpacking the single carrier she had brought aboard. The Inner Voice Communicator wasn't to be found. Agitated, she scattered the carrier's contents over the bed and sifted through it.

"Damn…" she swore aloud, "of all the stupid…! I forgot to remove the communicator from my robe pocket. Now I have no way of contacting Legend unless I use my transmitter and I don't dare take the chance of someone picking up my signal." She knew however he'd be aware something was wrong when she didn't check in as planned and would track her through Pragora's Chaser banks.

Breathing a sigh of frustrated resignation, she checked her watch. *Wonder what time they eat around here?*

As though intercepting her thoughts the control computer chimed, "The captain requests your presence on deck 4 at 1800 hours for dinner. You may take the vacuum lift located at the end of your corridor."

Jessica entered the marble tiled bathroom and splashed warm water over her face. Brushing back her shoulder length hair, she extended a portion over her temple to cover the small bandage. She weaved the rest into a plait and secured it with a leather thong from her bag then exited the bathroom, leaving the lights to extinguish themselves. She crossed the lounge and out the hatchway door to the waiting lift.

***

Vantra's informant had access to all areas of the ship, but since there were no diplomats aboard it might look suspicious for him to be in this area. It meant taking a risk, but from what Naal relayed he would be at greater risk if he failed. As long as Caldar kept to her schedule he could breathe easy, but there was always the chance of a mess up and he needed to be in a position to see that *that* didn't happen.

As Officer of Protocol, his assignment required him to escort all dignitaries aboard. Space Station Oron had requested that the Urieian Ambassador, and two of his officials, be transported up from Pragora and continue with the Glennden to Delta-Con-Seven. This fit his plans perfectly; he would personally escort Caldar to the transporter room while he received the dignitaries, and then transport her to her destination. *Not exactly the one she will be expecting though,* he thought.

The door across from Jessica's slid shut softly behind him as he snaked into the corridor in the opposite direction Jessica had taken.

***

Besides the captain and his second in command, four officers were seated at the table when Jessica arrived. As drinks were being served, a fifth officer appeared, made his apology for being late, and slipped into the empty seat next to hers. The general conversation centered around their current flight to Delta-Con-Seven.

The captain's table proved to be a pleasant surprise with its array of serving dishes and exotic flowers decking the center of the kidney shaped table. Most of the officers present hailed from various parts of the Galaxy, and "Cook" had simulated food accordingly.

"Compliments of the captain," he said, serving Jessica a savory dish of Silver-tipped Kropian basted in sweet wine and sprinkled with nuts soaked in blue cream.

After the course was finished, a variety of fruits and sweets were passed around, along with Moon Tea in tall slender glasses, laced with Cordoe from the planet Scorpra.

The tardy officer at Jessica's right broached the subject of her assignment.

"I understand you will be going into the caves of Pragora?"

Hoping to keep the conversation general, she replied, "Yes, it should prove interesting. I've never been to Pragora."

"It's my understanding," he persisted, "you've been assigned to search for Prince Vantra." He gazed around the table as though he were privy to something the others didn't know. "Do you think the Eternians might be holding him prisoner?"

Jessica was irritated with his questions and would have liked to tell him so, but realized it would only raise more questions.

"It's only speculation at the moment and a subject best left to Chaser officials," she answered briskly. The others seemed to understand and directed the conversation away to other matters. The rest of the evening passed pleasantly enough and when it came time to disperse she shook hands all around, thanked the captain for an excellent meal, and departed for her quarters.

***

"The time is now 0700," the control computer chimed. Have a pleasant morning."

Jessica stretched and yawned, feeling rested after a good night's sleep. She was hungry and eager for breakfast.

Slipping into the micro-shower she let the warm waves of energy soothe away the effects of her encounter with Protandel. She stepped out of the shower and inspected her face in the mirror. *I think this can go.* She yanked off the bandage at her temple and smoothed her fingers over the wound. *Probably going to leave a scar.* She finished dressing and moved out into the corridor hurrying to the mess hall.

The mess hall was empty except for First Officer Cordova. Cordova rose from his chair and stood behind it motioning for her to sit in the place he had just vacated.

"I apologize for not keeping you company, but I'm wanted on the bridge. He lowered his voice in a conspiratorial whisper. "I must warn you, Cook's been harboring some old cookbook he dug up from the ship's library last year. Every once in a while he tries out a new recipe on us. The others got wind of this new one and skipped out. The last time we tried one of his 'special meals' most of us spent the morning in the latrine. I suggest you make a quick exit."

"I assure you," Jessica whispered in return, checking to see if Cook was within earshot, not quite sure if the First Officer was serious, "I'm hungry enough to eat whatever Cook puts in front of me."

He chuckled and placed his cap on his head. "In that case I'll leave you to your fate. But don't say I didn't warn you." He moved through the hatchway and out of sight. Jessica sat wondering if maybe she should take Cordova's advice after all and retreat while she still had the chance. There was a simulator in her room and she could call up her own breakfast. She was about to make her escape when Cook entered carrying a tray. He glanced around and frowned shaking his head.

"Cowards," he mumbled. "No loyalty." He shuffled over to Jessica and set the tray down in front of her. "Well, little lady," he said, smiling mischievously, "it looks like you're the only brave one in the bunch." Nodding his head to indicate the tray, he asked, "Do you mind?"

Jessica looked up at him and chuckled. "Do I have a choice?"

Cook's eyes twinkled. "Don't you worry, miss. According to the book I found in the ship's library, this dish was pretty popular among the Early Earth people called, Americans. I have to admit it was no easy job gettin' that blasted simulator to duplicate the recipe, but here it is." He stepped back rubbing his big hands on the pristine apron covering his large frame. "Now you just take a bite of this and tell me what ya think."

"Well..." she said, trying to hide her amusement. "I believe it would be helpful if I had something to eat it with."

He laughed out loud. "You sure are right about that, little lady." He bent over and laid the fork he had been holding next to the tray.

Jessica picked it up and lifted a cautious sample of the unidentified morsel to her mouth, chewed a little, then smiled up at him. "I'd say you have a winner here." It was delicious and she wondered why it had become obsolete. "I'll bet the captain would love this," she said, shoveling in a mouthful this time. "It just might become a regular item again."

Cook flushed, his face beaming. "Do you really think so?"

"Yes, I *really* do."

With head held high, he marched into the other room and patted the simulator. "Wha'da ya know," he said proudly, "we've re-discovered chip beef on toast."

***

"May I show you around?" First Officer Cordova asked, as Jessica stepped through to the bridge. "Captain Twayne is in engineering, but I'd be happy to assist with any questions you might have."

"Thank you, I appreciate the offer, but I can see you're busy. I'll just browse on my own. That's if you don't mind?" she added.

"Feel free to go wherever you wish. The lift will take you to all levels of the ship. There are ten, counting engineering. You might find our library on deck 4 of interest. It's quite extensive and contains several books from the archives of Old Capital. Speaking of old books, did you sample Cook's American dish?"

"Yes, I did and I think you should try it yourself. It was very good."

"Really?" he said, arching an eyebrow.

"Really," she repeated seriously.

"Humm...then I'll see to it Cook is given free reign to endow us with his new concoction."

"I'm sure you'll enjoy it," she said smiling, then asked, "Do you mind if I look around the bridge?"

"Not at all. I'd like to be able to give you a firsthand account of what's going on, but I see I'm needed at the moment." He nodded towards a man beckoning to him. "If you'll excuse me." He left her side to stand before a virtual screen overlaid with navigational maps of the galaxy. Two crewmembers sat at monitors before the viewing port coding instructions into the main frame. It was all quite interesting, but Jessica felt out of her depth and decided to move on.

She took the lift to the library, a spacious combination of rooms, each designed to reflect its subject. Old Capital Room was mirrored with pictures depicting life as it must have been before the capital's destruction. Rare books lay open beneath glass casings, their pages brown and crinkled with age. Artifacts and statues, removed from the ruins, were positioned around the room. It was a museum in itself. *I wonder how Prince Vantra managed to get his hands on all this*, she thought, as she examined the precious items. *No doubt he used his power to fleece the Archives* of *Ancient History.*

Jessica visited two more decks. She was in the lift to level 8 when the control computer announced their arrival and immediate docking, adding, "Chaser Caldar, please meet Officer Brankton in the ship's lounge on deck 5 for transport to Zeer."

Oh no! Not him! she thought, remembering last night's dinner. *I wonder what questions I'll have to dodge this time.*

She retrieved her belongings and proceeded to the rendezvous. A slight jar of the ship informed her that the Glennden had docked at the space station. She entered the pleasantly festooned lounge where Officer Brankton was seated at a cube shaped table.

"Hello, we meet again." Rising, he extended his hand. "I'm here to see you safely transported to Zeer."

"I see," Jessica replied, reluctantly offering her own hand.

Avoiding her direct gaze, he glanced at his watch.

"I hope I've not delayed you?" she asked, noting his fidgeting.

"Not at all," he replied, clearing his throat. "I hope your quarters were satisfactory?" He smiled, but any warmth intended failed to register.

"I'm on my way to meet the Urieian ambassador," he continued, seemingly uninterested in her reply to his question. "Since you're unfamiliar with the ship I thought you might need an escort to the transporter room."

"Thank you, I appreciate your concern, but I think I could have managed."

Brankton shrugged and abruptly turned to lead the way to the waiting lift. "Transporter deck," he instructed the control computer as they entered.

They exited into a large well-lit room where two albino Marovians stood poised before virtual screens silently awaiting instructions for the transfer of the Urieian ambassador to the Glennden.

"Set coordinates," Brankton ordered.

The two nodded in unison as they began a series of graceful movements across the screens. A tangle of wiry brown hair hung over their extended brows, partially hiding eyes shielded beneath second lids. Enveloped in robes of deep red, it was impossible to distinguish their gender. Jessica turned to Brankton. "How are they able to understand you?"

"They have cranium implants," he answered. "The central computer translates our language into sounds compatible with their own. Motion holograms are received by their brain waves through the implants as well. Of course, this is all voluntary," he added.

"Interesting the way they move as one," Jessica commented, attracted by their graceful movements.

"We have twenty such pairs on board," he said. "They mate for life on their mother planet and are sealed together at an early age by what they call Au-Nu. Once they are 'sealed' one cannot survive without the other. If one dies the other dies as well, although, as a rule, they do live long lives. This race of aliens has proven to be very useful."

His patronizing undertone was not hidden from Jessica, as though these large beings, because they started from another life form, were good for nothing but workers. She was taking a very distinct dislike to Brankton.

"Transfer from Pragora beginning. Arrival in three seconds," the computer intoned.

"Good, that will be the ambassador," Brankton said.

Jessica's attention was drawn away from the Marovians to three life forms within the transparent cylinders of the transporters. Brankton stepped forward to receive the Urieian ambassador and his envoy. "Welcome, sir," he said, saluting. "May I introduce you to Chaser Caldar of the Federation. Jessica, this is Ambassador Aundara of the Urieian Council."

"My pleasure, sir," she said, saluting as well, before offering her hand.

"Chaser Caldar is transporting down to Pragora. Prince Vantra is missing and she's been ordered to investigate the caves," Brankton informed the ambassador.

Jessica shot him an annoyed glance.

"Yes, we were informed of his disappearance before we left Urie," replied Aundara. "It is most shocking." He turned to address Jessica. "We have relayed messages to your Council of Six assuring our support and help should they require them. Our association with the Federation is greatly valued. We wish you well in your search."

Before Jessica could respond, Brankton interrupted. "Sir, I'm sure you must be tired. I have an escort waiting to take you to your quarters."

Aundara looked directly at Jessica and nodded with a smile, ignoring Brankton's rudeness. "We mustn't detain our friend any longer from her duty. If you will be so kind." He motioned to Brankton, indicating he was now ready for the escort.

The hatch slid open at Brankton's signal and two waiting ensigns stepped forward, saluted and motioned for the ambassador and the others to precede them to the waiting lift.

He watched them depart then checked his watch. "Ready?"

Jessica stepped close to him. "First I want to know how you became so well informed of my mission?" Her voice was threatening.

He was visibly uncomfortable, but replied, "Captain Twayne advised me of your purpose here. As his third officer it's only natural I should be informed."

Jessica doubted that and wanted to question him further, but the computer had begun its countdown and she had to step into the waiting cylinder. *I think I'd better call up Captain Twayne when I get to headquarters.*

"Transfer," Brankton commanded.

A moment later, believing herself to be in Pragora's Chaser Headquarters, expecting to meet Jarod Krinner, Jessica instead found herself within a small barred cell. She stared in disbelief. Too late she saw the sneering face of Naal, his raised arm poised to strike. The blow fell with a sickening thud and a black cloak sheathed her in its lifeless embrace.

***

After Jessica's departure Legend accessed Chaser computer banks for information concerning Jarod Krinner. The file was surprisingly brief. It listed Krinner's excellent record and promotions. He entered Chaser training at the age of eighteen and was assigned to the outpost planet Zeer two years later. At age twenty-one he was re-assigned as Director of Operations to oversee the colonization of Pragora, now Intercept Headquarters for the Federation and a stopover for diplomats traveling within their galactic domain. But oddly there was no record of him before he entered the academy.

When ample time had passed and Jessica hadn't contacted him through the communicator as planned, Legend knew something was wrong. Accessing the Federation mainframe, he discovered she was missing and a search party had been dispatched to investigate the caves. Legend's console buzzed to life as a coded message threaded its way to a secret destination. *JESSICA MISSING, MAY BE IN CAVES.*

***

Previous to Legend's message, Jarod was on his visual. "Glennden, this is Jarod Krinner. What's the problem up there? You were supposed to transfer Chaser Caldar down here an hour ago."

"Sir, Officer Brankton sent her down at the specified time and coordinates. Our logs concur her departure time."

"Well check your logs again and have the computer run a second scan on the coordinates. Let me know as soon as you have them."

"Yes, sir. I'll relay your message to the captain. Glennden off."

Jarod pushed back his chair in irritation and rose from behind his desk away from the viewer screen. *Where the hell is she? I've wasted enough time.*

After a short interval the captain appeared on screen. "Captain Twayne here. Looks like we have a problem. Our ship's main computer picked up a slight distortion during Caldar's transfer. The computer is tracking it now, but the electrical storms created by your Black Moon are interfering with the signal. We think it may have been a tracker beam from the colony, but we can't be sure. We've been unable to pinpoint the precise location. The signal has faded over the past hour, but from what we've been able to trace, it looks as though it could have come from somewhere near the caves. I suggest you begin your own investigation. We'll do what we can here, but our departure for the Bora system and Delta-

Con-Seven is within the hour. We don't dare delay or we'll miss our orbit. I'll let you know if we find out anything before then. Captain Twayne off."

Jarod dropped into his chair, his strong features set in a deep frown, contemplating whether to notify Quad immediately or continue on his own until he had more information. Coming to a decision he went on screen.

"Quad, this is Jarod Krinner. Caldar never arrived at her assigned destination. It's possible her point of entry has been compromised."

"What the hell went wrong?" Quad asked, anger creasing his brows. "How did it happen? You were supposed to meet her when she transported down to headquarters."

"Hold on, Quad, that's just the point, she never arrived! If you'll give me half a chance I'll tell you what I've been able to find out so far."

"Okay, let's hear it," Quad snapped.

Jarod rose from his chair and started pacing, his mood dark. "According to Captain Twayne his third officer transported her down as scheduled. They aren't certain, but she may have been intercepted by a tracker beam. He says they'll keep checking their computer data, but they've got to leave the space station within the hour. Is it possible she might have made arrangements with someone else to get her into the caves?"

"No," Quad answered emphatically. "Jessica may not like the idea of working with someone else, but she's dependable. She's been pretty much a loner ever since her father's death, but she would never disobey an order. You'd better get on this right away. In the meantime I'm coming up. The next flight to Zeer connects with the space station in eighteen hours; I'll be on it. And Jarod, Augueen and the boys are due in at the same time. I told her to contact you when their ship docks. I'd appreciate it if you'd make arrangements for someone to meet them."

"I'll see that she's in good hands."

"Then expect me in a few hours. Off."

"Commander Taybor," Jarod instructed the computer as soon as Quad had switched off. "If he's not in his quarters, try base flight control. Tell him I'd like to see him in my office as soon as he can make it. End of message."

Kraft Taybor was Space Commander of Zeer's Pragora Base. He and Jarod had been friends long before either had signed up for their particular fields. Kraft signed on as an ensign with the galactic star cruiser, Aurora, the same time Jarod entered cadet training as a Chaser. Both, to their mutual pleasure, ended up on Pragora nine years later.

"What's up?" Kraft asked, entering Jarod's office an hour later, flopping his short, stocky frame into a nearby chair. "I gathered from your message you've got more on your mind than a chat with an old buddy?"

"I need you for some reconnaissance," Jarod replied. "I'd like you to fly me over the caves. One of my fellow Chasers has come up missing and from all indications may have been intercepted by a tracker beam on the way down from the Glennden. At least that's what the captain thinks and I'm inclined to agree, except it is possible this may have been Caldar's plan all along. I understand she wasn't too happy having to hook up with me."

"She?" asked Kraft, a sly grin breaking over his square jaw.

"Yes, she," Jarod repeated. "And wipe that grin off your ugly face. Maybe she'll be your type. I'll see what I can do to set you up."

"Whoa there!" Kraft raised both hands as though warding off an attack. "You know I'm a confirmed bachelor."

Jarod laughed. "That's what you claim every time you get cornered."

"And what makes you think I've ever been cornered?"

"Well let's see, there was GeNor, Tress..."

Kraft squirmed in his chair. "Okay, okay...but is it my fault they got the wrong impression."

"Funny, that's not what they said when they came crying on my shoulder," Jarod said.

Kraft cleared his throat. "All right, so let's get back to the subject at hand."

"I thought we were."

"Dammit, Jarod, you know what I mean!"

Jarod chuckled, enjoying Kraft's discomfort.

Kraft ignored Jarod's attempt to rile him. Pushing up from his chair, he asked, "When do you want to head out?"

"Soon as we can," Jarod replied, turning serious as he seated himself once again behind his desk.

"Might be wise to wait for Red Moon's zenith, even if the weather is freezing," Kraft suggested. "Should provide enough light to cruise low without being observed. I think we can scan the area thoroughly before Black Moon obscures the terrain. Let's see," Kraft lifted his arm glancing at his watch. "Red Moon will be up in approximately two hours, I'll wait for you on the flight pad. I've been looking for an excuse to get you up in my new star flyer. She's a beaut. See you then, pal," he said, throwing a back handed wave as he departed out the door.

"Access data," Jarod instructed the computer after Kraft left. "Confirm arrival time of cruiser from Borkia and check the passenger list to be sure Augueen Mossu and sons are aboard."

Following a brief pause, the computer responded, "Cruiser flight Trojan from Dadessery quadrant departed Borkia 10 a.m. yesterday. Arrival 8:05 interstellar time sixteen hours from now. Passenger Augueen Mossu and two sons confirmed as being aboard. Further instructions?"

Jarod rubbed his thumb over the rough texture of his chin. *Humm…feels like sandpaper.* "Message to Slade Dermott at Intercept Headquarters. Need a favor. Sign it Jarod. Off."

Chapter 11
The Search

Zeer's Pragorian colony, surrounded by a terrain of wastelands and swamps, became important for its crystal buried deep within rocky mounds. The valuable commodity was used for trade with Federation allies, but newer and stronger alloys were discovered on other planets and after several decades the crystal became obsolete. The colony, however, continued to thrive. Many of New Earth's people, tired of living beneath domed cities, volunteered to live on Pragora. Now, twenty years later, Pragora was an important way-station for diplomats traveling within her galactic domain.

***

"What did I tell ya," Kraft said. "Ain't she somethin'?"

Jarod and Kraft were seated in the sleek star flyer's interior.

"A bit snug, don't you think?" Jarod remarked, shifting his muscular frame in the cramped cockpit.

"She may be small," Kraft replied, "but she's well equipped." He turned and arced his hand over the instrument screen and finger tapped several digital displays, activating the controls. "I've set the Sound Refractors," he said. "That'll allow us to approach the caves without being heard."

"We'll still be vulnerable within the BorCron's sensor fields. Without proper authorization they'll fire on us," Jarod said.

"Not to worry, pal, I told you she's got everything."

"It's the 'not to worry' part I'm afraid of," Jarod responded, less than enthusiastic.

Kraft chuckled and touched one of the digital displays. "She's also equipped with an Impulse Defuser. The BorCrons sensors won't be able to pick us up. We'll keep in Red Moon's shadow on their blind side. Now if you don't have any more questions, I'll get us off the ground, unless, of course, you'd rather sit here jawing."

Jarod mockingly saluted Kraft. "You're the captain, Captain."

Kraft lifted the flyer off the pad. "Where do you want to start searching?" he asked. "The tunnels run in several directions."

"Let's begin above the entrance and work our way southward," Jarod answered.

"Gotcha," Kraft responded, tapping the instrument screen.

They passed over the airbase and headed south along the Lower Pragorian wasteland until they reached a cluster of deserted barracks surrounded by an electrode fence. A dome-covered gravity tube, previously used by the crystal miners to access the tunnels, ran above ground for a hundred feet, then disappeared into a rock wall rising several hundred feet above ground. The BorCron Directive held the computerized key that accessed the gravity tube.

Kraft turned to Jarod. "We're approaching the entrance. I'm activating the defuser till we're out of their sensor range."

A group of BorCrons milled around the entrance below, their black breastplates and helmets reflecting a metallic shadowy red glow in the moon's light. Others moved back and forth around its perimeter or strode to the building housing the giant generators left operable by the Council. A sweeper pod stood nearby, its rotating arms motionless above the steel body attached to floater tracts. The BorCrons gave no indication they were aware of the silent star flyer.

"Have you ever seen one of those things without its helmet?" Kraft asked as they passed over the site.

"No," Jarod answered. "Since there aren't any BorCrons on Zeer, except for the few Vantra sends up to guard the caves I've never really given them much thought."

"Well I have," Kraft said. "And it's not a pretty sight. On the Aurora I was given the job of cataloging the Eternian prisoners being transported here to Pragora. You know, scientists, computer biologists, that sort of thing.

"There was this guy with silver hair leaning against the bulkhead one day when I went in to finish the logging. Before I knew what happened he shoved me aside and grabbed the BorCron behind me around the neck and dragged him into the room. He managed to slam the bulkhead door on the others while several of the Eternians braced themselves against the door holding it shut.

"The man told me his name was Kell, that he was the Eternian's protector. He spoke to the others in a language I couldn't understand. It made the hairs at the back of my neck stand on edge. I can't explain it even now, but I knew Kell was not what he appeared to be. His eyes were the strangest blue

I'd ever seen and when they met mine over the shoulder of the BorCron he said, 'See what your Prince Vantra has created,' and pulled off the man's helmet. God, it was a monstrosity. A face covered with blackish tumors and malignant eyes that bulged out of their sockets, oozing gray matter every time he blinked, which was often."

"No wonder Vantra keeps them covered..." Jarod exclaimed.

"That's not all," Kraft continued. "Kell told me how they were created. Everyone knows Vantra cloned his Council of Six. That's no secret. But Kell revealed to me how Vantra's scientists were manipulating human genes and experimenting on 'em. Some of their experiments went bad, but rather than completely dispose of their failures they used their DNA to create these genetically engineered freaks. It's no wonder the Eternians fought against Vantra if these BorCrons are any example of his so-called *Enlightenment*."

Kraft guided the flyer over the rocky mound skirting its southern edge. The iridescent light from Red Moon sent eerie shadows across the ridges of the mound as they changed course to inspect the arm branching off to their left.

The flyer's heat sensors signaled movement beneath the surface and Kraft broke off his story.

"What's that?" Jarod asked, leaning towards Kraft to study the screen.

"Don't know. I'll just make this adjustment..." He tapped the screen. "Might be one of those tunnel feeder rats left behind by the crystal miners. But look at the size of that thing," he whistled. "Must be over three feet long. Never saw one that big," he said mystified. "Or moving that fast. They've lived in those caves over a hundred years now feeding on the local population of ground worms and spinners. Secretion from the worms was destroying the crystal and the spinners were poisonous to the men so the company purchased tunnel feeder rats from Alothos to keep them under control. The damn things must have mutated over the years," Kraft said, turning his head to look quizzically at Jarod.

"We may meet up with a few of those creatures if we have to search inside the caves," Jarod responded. "Unless we find something soon."

Kraft set their course to follow the northern perimeter, which would take them over the swamps.

"So finish your story," Jarod said. "What happened next?"

"This Kell guy opened the door and shoved me out along with the BorCron. There was retaliation for their actions, but you know, Jarod, I think they felt it was worth it to expose Vantra. I don't know. Maybe they thought I could help or something. The next day when I checked the log against the head count ten of the Eternians were unaccounted for. I was told without any explanation to mark 'em off the log. I never found out what happened, but I'd be willing to bet Kell was not one of 'em. It's possible he could be in the caves even now. Which brings up the question, where the hell are the Eternians? We should have picked up their heat patterns a long time ago. With that many people moving about they'd be impossible to miss."

"There's a lot going on here that doesn't add up," Jarod replied. "How could that many people just vanish, Caldar included?"

They glided silently over the swamp, passing over giant snails and swamp eels, without any sign of human life forms.

"Black moon will be up soon," Kraft said. "Its electric storms will disrupt my instruments. I'm sorry, Jarod, I know how important this is to you, but we'll have to wait until tomorrow to continue."

Jarod stared out the window. When he spoke his voice was somber. "As soon as I can get permission from the BorCron Directive I'm going inside the caves. If Caldar is in there I'll find her. And the Eternians as well."

Chapter 12
Prisoner

Jessica's hand felt heavy as lead as she pressed it to the base of her skull. Pain lanced her head, like shards of exploding glass. She heard a muffled groan and realized it was her own. *I must not be dead. I hurt too much,* she thought, shifting her body.

"About time you came to," a gruff, disembodied voice growled.

Her eyes wavered from side to side beneath their closed sockets then flicked open. She felt as though her stomach might yield up its contents any moment and clamped them shut again, lying motionless.

"I'm not impressed," the impatient voice persisted.

Before she could muster up the courage to open her eyes again, the voice rasped in anger, "Enough!"

A pair of rough hands jerked her erect to a sitting position.

Her eyes shot open. *Not a pretty sight,* she thought, staring into the face of the man standing over her. He was huge, hairy, and very ugly.

He lowered his head close to hers. His breath wafting over

her face smelled like something devoid of life. She attempted to turn her head away, but he clamped her chin between his thumb and fingers forcing her face upward.

"Don't like my pretty face, huh? Well you better get used to it 'cause you're gonna see a lot of it. Who knows, you may grow to love it." He tossed back his head and laughed, exposing sharp-edged teeth between thick lips. His long beard, woven into two braids beneath his extended jaw, brushed across her face. Jessica winced.

He moved away from her and strode across the room chuckling to himself. Jessica scrutinized the situation and weighed her chances of overpowering him, but that was out of the question. He stood almost seven feet tall and had the advantage of weapons, which she knew from the feel of her empty belt, she did not. Her eyes shifted over the room taking in her side pack, its contents scattered over the floor. An electrode force field that could disintegrate anything passing through it barred her prison.

"Okay," she said, "maybe you don't have the prettiest face in the universe, but what I want to know is, just why was I brought here?" Her head throbbed and she fought back the urge to vomit, but her voice rang strong as she continued. "Who the hell are you anyway, and what do you want with me?"

He leaned against the cell wall and folded his hairy arms. Jessica noted the spiral blades and knives nestled into the leather straps crisscrossing his broad chest. He smiled, but she knew it wasn't because he found her amusing.

"They call me Naal if you must know. As to what I want with you, *I* don't want anything. But then it's not me you need to worry about."

Jessica sensed he was toying with her. She also felt she wasn't going to get any straight answers from this overgrown hairball. She decided to bide her time and see what developed. It came sooner than expected.

"Good, Naal, I see you're keeping our prisoner entertained."

Jessica stiffened. Rising slowly to her feet she turned to face the man she had been sent to find. "It would seem," she said in a low, calm voice, not giving way to the trauma of her injuries, "you are not missing after all. What a pity."

Vantra's expression darkened, his wide brows knit together as he watched Jessica from beyond the force field. "Pity, Jessica Caldar, is what you'll be asking for after I let Naal spend time instructing you in the fine art of pain. He's very good at it in case you have any doubts. That is, unless of course..." he let the words elongate off his tongue, "you would care to cooperate...in which case I assure you no harm will come to you..."

"You mean like the Eternians?" she asked tauntingly. "And just how am I supposed to cooperate? I have no idea why I was brought here—wherever here is—in the first place, and even less what you have to do with all this." She motioned, indicating her prison, as well as Naal standing mute across the room. "I was sent by your Council of Six to discover your whereabouts. Instead I find myself your prisoner."

Vantra smiled malevolently, his voice smooth. "Ryden Caldar was stubborn too. I hope we don't have to use the same method of persuasion on his daughter, but then Ryden was weak and I'm afraid my friend here," Vantra glared at Naal, "lost his patience. Your father undermined me at every turn, but thanks to his lab assistant, I found out about the portal he was using to help the Eternians escape. Unfortunately, he died before we could discover its whereabouts."

"So you blew up his lab to make it look like an accident!" Jessica bolted for Vantra, fury blinding her to the force field. Naal sprang to intercept her, gripping her around the throat with a stranglehold. Jessica couldn't breathe. She tore at Naal's hands, but unconsciousness swept over her and she fell limp against the big man.

Vantra disengaged the force field and stepped inside the cell. "If you've killed her, you stupid fool, I'll have my guards tear the hide off you and nail it to the wall! She may be our only lead!" Vantra was enraged, he knew if he lost Jessica her father's secret would die with her.

"She's not dead, just unconscious," Naal responded, his brows lowered over a cold stare. "I'm well aware of her importance to you. I could have let her disintegrate herself, but I don't think that would serve your purpose." His tone was close to threatening.

Vantra was taken aback. He felt vulnerable without his guards. *Naal is becoming a dangerous liability,* he thought to himself. *I'll have to do something about that.* "Bring her around," he ordered. "I'm not finished with her yet."

Naal lifted Jessica from the floor and dropped her onto the cot. He slapped her several times on the cheeks then shook her till her eyes blinked open. Vantra pushed Naal aside and stood over Jessica. "Now where were we? I believe you were going to tell me where the portal is?"

Jessica smoothed a hand over her throat. Her voice was raspy. "I don't know, and even if I did, I'd never tell you, you murderer! I'd die before I'd tell you anything!"

Vantra struck her hard across the face. "We'll see about that, Caldar. After you've had a taste of isolation and hunger, you'll be more pliable." He turned away and stepped through the deactivated force field, barking at Naal. "Leave the bitch to her solitude."

Naal followed, reactivating the force field, leaving Jessica to ponder her fate. She slid from the bunk, her eyes straining to see what lay beyond the force field. One dim light penetrated the gloom. *Bide your time,* she thought. *Wait for an opening.*

***

Jarod and Kraft descended in a float pattern to the flight pad below. At the instant of touchdown Jarod jumped from the craft and strode with determined steps towards his waiting cruiser.

"Hey, hold up, buddy," Kraft yelled, sprinting across the field in Jarod's wake. "I'm going with you." Jarod turned and held up his hands as if to ward Kraft off, but Kraft only grinned. "No use trying to shake me off, pal, you got my adrenaline going and I'm not gonna be that easy to get rid of."

Jarod frowned and turned away, but, as though having second thoughts, turned back with a slight grin. "I should know by now you never know when to butt out."

It was late when they arrived at Chaser headquarters and Jarod's visual signaled an incoming message from Quad, aboard the New Venture.

"The Council of Six has ordered you to stand down until I arrive. If Caldar is in the caves she knows how to take care of herself, at least for the time being anyway. It seems the Council is concerned you may create problems in negotiations with the BorCron Directive for access to the caves. Let's just say they believe you're not noted for your diplomatic skills. Anyway, I will be arriving in just a few hours. I expect to find you at headquarters. Quad out."

Jarod swung angrily away from the screen. "Damn them all to—"

"Easy now," Kraft interrupted, knowing full well the barrage of words Jarod had in mind. "Maybe that's not such a bad idea. At this point you don't even know if she *is* in the caves. I know…" Kraft continued, raising his hands in a gesture of impatience as Jarod threatened to interrupt, "waiting is not your strongest asset."

Jarod scowled and sat on the edge of his desk, wishing for once Kraft would mind his own business instead of being so ready with advice. "And just what are we supposed to do in the meantime?" he asked mockingly. "Hope that whoever is holding her will entertain her until we can rescue her?"

Kraft retorted, "There's nothing we can do but wait like Quad said, and I, for one, am gonna catch some shuteye. It wouldn't hurt you either from the looks of you. A bit on the down side of shady, I'd say." As he headed for the door he turned and sent a parting shot. "And try shaving for once, will ya?" Something solid came whizzing past his head and bounced off the frame to his left. "Now that's what I call friendship," he snickered, and ducked out the door before Jarod had a chance to express more of the same.

Jarod slid behind his desk and instructed the computer to open a holofile of the caves. He hadn't been in them for quite some time, ever since Prince Vantra required special orders from the Directive to access. The mining company, however, had carefully mapped the labyrinth of tunnels, as well as the subterranean cavities, before the crystals had no longer become marketable. *I suppose Quad's right, Caldar can probably take care of herself, but I still need to pinpoint possible places she could have been taken.*

He opened the file, unaware that Vantra had concealed the cell where Jessica was being held, having had it erased from the file.

***

"Jarod!" Kraft shook the sleeping man. "Wake up! Chief Quad's here." Kraft shook him again. "Hey, buddy, this wasn't what I meant by getting some shuteye. Wake up, the man is waiting."

Jarod raised his head off his arms. "Wha…t?"

"I said, Chief Quad is in the outer office, now get your tired butt out'a this chair and get to it."

Jarod groaned. "What time is it?"

"Past eight; you're a sorry sight if ever I saw one. If I had time I'd dump you in the pond outside."

Jarod leaned back from his desk and brushed his fingers through his tousled hair. "Must'a fallen asleep."

"No kiddin'," Kraft responded. "Com'on, you'd better not keep him waiting. He was on a short fuse when I left him."

Jarod slipped from behind his desk, stretched and pulled at his disheveled uniform. He strode to the door with Kraft close behind. Quad was pacing the outer office, his face stormy.

"What the hell is going on? I was shuffled in here like some dim-witted cadet. You look like hell, Jarod."

"I fell asleep at my desk last night. I wasn't notified until now that your ship had docked."

"That's obvious," Quad sneered. "What about Augueen and the boys? I hope you made the arrangements I asked for."

Jarod looked unflinchingly at Quad. "They're at Intercept Headquarters. Now if you don't mind I think the current problem is Chaser Caldar."

Kraft grinned, enjoying the tension between the two. Jarod shot him a piercing glance. Kraft cleared his throat, rolled his eyes and looked away. Annoyed, Jarod jerked open the door and motioned Quad through into his office.

The Borkian dropped into the nearest chair, his lidless eyes cold. A strained silence filled the room as Jarod seated himself behind his desk and waited for the big man to speak. Kraft sauntered over to the window, leaned his stocky frame against its glass and folded his arms across his chest. A slight grin creased his lips; he was enjoying himself at the expense of these two.

Quad broke the silence, his gravelly voice held an edge to it. "What have you learned from Captain Twayne?"

Jarod responded in like manner. "Nothing. It looks like we're on our own."

Quad grunted. "Well, what have you done so far?"

Jarod leaned forward bracing his arms on the desktop, his gray eyes intent. "Look, Quad, I'm not your flunky and this isn't your planet. If we're going to work together let's do it *together* or you can get someone else for the job!"

Quad jerked upright, his hands flat on the desk. Jarod watched unflinching. Thinking Quad intended to grab Jarod and pull him over the desk, Kraft stiffened, dropped his arms, and pushed away from the window. Quad stood fixed for a moment, his expression unreadable. Then suddenly he relaxed and extended his four-fingered hand.

"Yes, of course, you're right. Finding Jessica is the issue here."

Jarod, as surprised as Kraft at this sudden change, pulled himself up from the desk, paused for a moment, then accepted Quad's hand.

"Now," Quad said, sitting back down as though the incident hadn't transpired between them, "fill me in on what's happened so far."

Jarod nodded towards Kraft who was once again relaxed against the window. "Commander Taybor flew me over the caves, but nothing human showed up on the heat sensors.

Not even the Eternians, which is equally strange. My gut feeling is somehow there's a connection. If Captain Twayne's figures are correct, and I have no reason to believe otherwise, that tracker beam came from the caves or nearby. The only other possible place would be the empty miner's barracks. I figure we should start there first then take the gravity tube into the caves themselves."

Quad stood. "I'll make arrangements with the BorCron Directive to shut down the force field surrounding the barracks. We can start the search tomorrow. Right now I'm going to see to my wife and sons. Where can I find them?"

Jarod assigned one of his aides to accompany Quad to Intercept Headquarters while he showered and shaved. Then he and Kraft reviewed the holofile of the caves.

Intercept Headquarters was a series of buildings set in the middle of the Pragorian colony. Its structure consisted of transparent aluminum, filtering out the damaging rays of Zeer's sun, as well as radiating a constant controlled temperature suitable for the work force.

The planet's two moons presented challenges, their cycles lasting up to six hours. Red Moon brought with it temperatures of eighty below despite its deceptive warm glow. Without thermo suits, men could freeze solid in thirty minutes. The strange array of intropeds which inhabited the planet had adapted, entering a phase of hibernation during Red Moon's cycle. Their eyeless bodies had evolved into giant eel-like creatures that inhabited the swamps. Black Moon, following in its wake, created electrical storms and darkness so deep that without lights it was impossible to see your hand in front of your face.

Several rooms within Intercept Headquarters were reserved for high officials and dignitaries transferring to the space station as they awaited ships to their various destinations. Seated in one of these rooms were Quad's wife, Augueen, and their two young sons, Condee and Retsel.

Augueen rose and moved restlessly across the carpeted floor. Her full-length gown of blue silk rustled as she stepped to the window, a look of concern in her lidless amber flecked eyes. A cap of dark curls framed her oval face.

Between the two boys nestled a small cat-like creature called a mocker. From time to time it would stretch its furry body and twitter in a language similar to that of the Borkian's. Condee and Retsel were restless and started jostling each other, their giggles growing louder as they pushed and shoved. Augueen turned and spoke to them in their native tongue, a series of clicks and hums. The boys, chastised, ceased their antics and turned their attention back to their pet. The animal stretched and twittered mocking Augueen's voice. The boys giggled.

Augueen picked up the gentle creature and rubbed her hand over its soft green fur then set it back between her sons. It twittered and curled up in a ball. "You've taught Poom well," she said in Borkian. "Sometimes I think too well." A smile tweaked the corners of her mouth.

The door swung open and Quad strode into the room sweeping Augueen into his arms. The boys jumped from their chairs and grabbed both parents around the hips. Everyone was clicking, humming and laughing.

"English now," Quad said sternly. "You're on Federation soil." Smiling, he dropped his hands to the boys' shoulders and gave them a squeeze.

"It's been so long," Augueen said, her voice soft without the gravelly Borkian speech.

"I know. I've missed you," Quad responded, lifting his hands from the boys to grip hers. "How is your mother?"

"She is not well. I fear her health is much deteriorated. But she would not hear of me staying longer. Sadar assured me she would give her the best of care and I was not to worry. She is such a faithful servant and devoted to Mother. I know I have left her in good hands, but still..." Augueen lowered her eyes and sighed, then raised them again to meet her husband's. A moist tear rested on one cheek. She smiled wanly and asked, "When do we return to New Earth? I'm afraid the boys have become quite restless and they are anxious to see their friends."

Quad smoothed the tear away with his thumb. "It may be a few more days," he answered, his expression serious. "Jessica Caldar is missing and we believe she may have been taken into the crystal caves."

Augueen put her hand to her mouth. "Oh, Quad, that's terrible. How did it happen?"

Quad moved Augueen to a chair and sat next to her explaining the events that led up to Jessica's disappearance.

"But I want to go back to New Earth," sniffled Retsel, the younger of the two.

"You said we could go home tomorrow," Condee scolded.

"Quiet, boys," Quad admonished. "I must look for our friend, Jessica."

Augueen smiled tenderly at them. "I know it's hard, but who knows, you might find some new friends here." She turned back to Quad and touched his cheek. "Do whatever you must and don't worry about us, we will be fine."

Quad's rough features softened as he kissed her and brushed a hand over her dark curls.

Chapter 13
Harm's Way

Kraft set the hyper-cruiser down close to one of the empty barracks. As the three men alighted a blast of icy wind whirled around their thermo suits.

"Hard to realize how cold Pragora can get, considering the surrounding desert," Jarod said, his breath expelled in a vaporous cloud.

"I wonder how those BorCron guards keep from freezin'." Kraft said. "Must be somethin' added to their DNA when they were cloned."

Jarod tapped him on the shoulder and pointed to the barracks. "Why don't you check them out while Quad and I unload the gear?"

Kraft lifted a flashlight from inside the cruiser and headed for the nearest building. The door squealed on rusted hinges as he pushed it open and stepped inside. Flipping on the flashlight, he moved the beam along the walls then up to the ceiling where steel rafters ran the full length of the barracks. Narrow windows, crusted over with film, were embedded high on both sidewalls. Bunks, rusted and falling apart, once used by the crystal miners, were stacked in tiers of three on each side of a wide central isle. Several bunks had toppled from the upper ties to the floor below.

When he checked out the toilets and shower stalls at each end of the hall he found them green with algae and smelling of mold and old urine.

Kraft headed back towards the entrance, the beam of his flashlight moving ahead along the puddle soaked floor. His footfalls echoed like claws on metal as he traversed the littered aisle. He paused, but the sound continued. "What-the...." He swung the beam of his light back along the aisle and stood listening. A low growl sounded high to his left. As he swung the beam upward towards the sound, a flash of grey disappeared into the shadows. Kraft continued along the aisle cautious now, straining to see what lay beyond the shadows. He heard a screech just as the thing launched itself from one of the top bunks. Raising his hands to protect his face he felt the slash of sharp claws across his arm. The flashlight flew from his grasp and he staggered backwards hitting one of the cots. His legs buckled under him and he fell hard onto his side. Scrambling upright, he released his laser from its holster and crouched, squinting into the dark. The flashlight rolled in a circle sending weird shadows up and down the aisle. He retrieved the light and slowly pivoting his body, scanned the rows of rusting cots. Nothing moved. An icy cold began to steal upward towards his shoulder. The sleeve of his thermo suit was ripped open from elbow to shoulder and blood from his wound was dripping to the floor.

"Come on, wherever you are, try it again!" he yelled into the shadows. "Let's see how you like a taste of laser for your meal!" He slowly backed towards the door. Resting the flashlight on his weapon, he swung it from side to side, his eyes darting in every direction. A low growl came from beneath a row of cots to his right. He swung around and fired his laser several times. A loud screech pierced the air, then silence. Kraft squinted, but couldn't see anything. His back bumped against the door. Reaching behind him, he slowly lifted the latch. Wham! The thing hit the door just above his knees, fangs clicking wildly. Kraft jerked the door open pinning the thing against the wall. It screamed in rage, its red eyes blazing, as Kraft raised his laser and fired.

"We heard shots," Jarod yelled, running into the building, Quad close at his heels. "What's happened?"

Kraft, his face pale, pulled back the door and the gray body dropped to the floor.

"What...the."

"I think we know now what a tunnel feeder looks like," he said, glancing from Jarod to Quad.

Quad turned the dead rat over with the toe of his boot. "This thing's gotta be at least three feet long."

"Yeah, big and nasty," Kraft said. "Think I may need some patchin' up." He lifted his good arm and fingered the ripped sleeve. Blood dripped off the end of his fingertips.

Jarod looked concerned. "We'd better get back to the cruiser and take care of that before infection sets in."

"What'll we do with this?" Kraft asked, prodding the limp carcass.

"Leave it," Quad answered. "We've got enough to worry about. It's not going anywhere."

Returning to the cruiser, Jarod helped Kraft out of his thermo jacket. The wound went deep and would have to be cleaned and cauterized. He took out the Med-Pac and poured a cleansing agent over the wound to ward off infection. Then he set his laser to its lowest setting.

"Hold still, will ya!"

"I am, dammit!" Kraft flared, his lips compressed into a grimace. "Will you just get on with it!"

Jarod slowly drew the laser beam across the wound, cauterizing and closing it.

Kraft let out a string of profanity and glared at Jarod. "You're enjoying this!" he growled.

Jarod chuckled and handed Kraft a spare jacket from the supply crate. "Com'on, pal, you've been through worse than this. How about that scar you're carrying across your ribs, the one you got fighting those war ships from Goli. Tell you what," he said slyly, "if I lose it with one of those tunnel feeders you can have at it."

"I'll see what I can do," Kraft scowled, yanking at his jacket as he alighting from the cruiser.

Jarod stepped to his side. "What's the deal on the building?"

"That's more important than the walking wounded?" Kraft asked. His voice edgy.

"I think you'll live," Jarod quipped, laying a hand on his good shoulder.

Kraft swung around causing Jarod's hand to slide off, his look cold. "What the hell's that supposed to mean?"

"Okay, pal, what's going on with you? I've never seen you so tense."

Kraft brushed past Jarod, grazing his shoulder as he went. "What the hell do you know about it?" He stalked away, dust rolling up from his boots.

Jarod was mystified by his friend's outburst. It wasn't like Kraft to take him so seriously, or flare up like that.

"What's gotten into him?" Quad asked, walking up to Jarod.

"Nothing," Jarod answered, watching Kraft's retreating back. "Nothing. Let's get the gear stored. We don't have time to check the rest of the buildings."

When Kraft joined them later his black mood seemed to have passed, although he appeared quiet and subdued. When asked if he needed help setting up the computer they had brought, he simply shook his head and proceeded on his own.

Quad took a turn around the barracks, laser in hand, searching for any tunnel feeders that might be in hiding. "I think that was a loner," he said. "At least I hope so."

"Well, if there are any left this should take care of 'em," Kraft said, motioning towards the computer. "I've programmed in a thermo scan with a force field perimeter that will eliminate anything non-human." His lips bent in an exaggerated grin. "I suggest, Quad, you remember to stay well beyond the perimeter once it's set."

Quad looked suspiciously at Kraft, not liking the way he was staring back at him. "Thanks...I'll remember."

Jarod, not privy to the exchange, strolled up and announced, "Since we don't know how long we'll be in the caves, we'd better take food-packets and water flasks. Everything else can be sealed in the aluminum crate."

They attached the supply crate to pulley cables suspended from the rafters. The cables were equipped with electrode trips to discourage any rats stowing aboard.

"We'd better use these," Jarod said, strapping a vid-com to his wrist and handing one to each man. "They're linked to the computer and will keep us in communication with each other as well as coordinating our position should we get separated. Keep your lasers handy. Once we're out of the gravity tube, we don't know how many of those rats we might meet up with. They've had a long time to breed."

"Wonder how that one got out of the caves?" Quad commented.

"Probably dug its own tunnel to the barracks," Jarod responded. "I wonder how many more have tunneled their way through to the other buildings. At least we'll be ready this time."

Kraft rubbed his injured arm, his eyes glazed over. "Yeah."

Chapter 14
Escape

Jessica licked her dry chapped lips. She lay on a cot in a fetal position, thirsty and hungry. *What was it, two, three days since she had been taken captive?* She pulled the single blanket closer hoping it would provide some warmth. Strength was slowly being sapped from her body and she wondered how long she could last if she didn't get something to eat soon. *Food, water, water, food,* they alternated at the vortex of her mind, swimming in a sea of confusion. Would she go insane before she died? Where was Naal? Even the promised pain would be better than this. At least it would assure her she was still alive. Fear ballooned like a spidery web through her brain, its silken thread stretching ever thinner. It was the first time she had experienced such fear. Not of dying, but dying like *this*. With Evaders at least she stood a chance.

"I see you're more docile. Not so arrogant now that you've had time to think about your situation." Naal's voice sliced through the web drawing her back to reality. "Shall I bring *his highness* here so you can plead with him to spare you before I begin...?"

Jessica remained mute.

"No? Well then..." His voice lowered to a whispered threat as he advanced closer to her cot. "I'll just enjoy having you to myself for a while."

She lay with her back to him. Sensing his approach her muscles tensed. *Just a little closer...*

"I hope you're not dead yet," he said, whispering into her ear.

Jessica fought back the urge to move her cramped legs from their fetal position as heat flamed through every muscle. Feeling Naal's sour breath as he bent over her, Jessica struck. Both legs shot out from under the blanket, her feet connecting with Naal's knees. A sharp *crack* told her she had guessed right. Naal screamed obscenities as he dropped to the floor, his face an agony of pain. Jessica rolled off the opposite side of the cot but her legs buckled beneath her and she collapsed in a heap. Grasping the cot for support, she hauled herself upright to her knees. Prickling pain radiated up her legs, but she struggled to a standing position. She had to get to Naal before he sounded an alarm. Pulling at the cot for support, she slowly made her way around to where he was writhing on the floor. She slid to the floor and made a grab for one of the knives sheathed in his armor straps. Naal tried to knock her hand away, but pain slowed his action and she yanked the knife free. Her intention was to hold it to his throat and force him to open the force field, but Naal suddenly swung his huge body over hers pinning her beneath him. The knife held between their bodies plunged deep into his chest. His eyes widened in disbelief as he tried to cry out, but the blade had been driven through his heart. He raised an arm as though to strike, but it fell away limp as he drew a rasping breath and collapsed on top of her. Jessica struggled to push him off and onto his back. Blood pooled around the protruding knife. His eyes were glassy staring at the ceiling. Trembling and weak, Jessica crawled backwards on her buttocks until she came in contact with the cot. Burying her face in the blanket her body shook with sobs.

Time was slipping away. She had to make her escape before someone discovered Naal and sounded the alarm. Jessica crawled back to his body. Avoiding looking into his lifeless eyes, she removed two daggers from one of the armor straps and tucked them into her waist belt then probed for the deactivator. But it wasn't in any of his pockets. She strained to roll Naal's limp body onto its side. The embedded knife made a soft *clink* as it made contact with the floor. The deactivator lay wedged beneath him. Jessica slipped it out and sat back on her haunches to catch her breath. *Gotta get out of here.* Using the cot for support, she pulled herself erect. Circulation gradually returned to her legs. Forcing herself away from the cot, she staggered to the force field and opened it with the deactivator and slipped into the dimly lit corridor.

Back pressed against the wall, hands splayed at her sides, Jessica threaded her way along the central corridor, its surface smooth and cool to the touch. *Some kind of metal,* she thought.

Her progress was infuriatingly slow, her body objecting to every movement. At one point dizziness threatened to overtake her, the corridor ahead wavering as though she were submerged in water. She paused, waiting for the dizziness to pass. Several feet ahead the corridor split off into two separate passageways; Jessica chose the one to her left. She had gone only a few steps when she was startled by the sound of an airlock. Light flooded the passageway ahead of her as two dark forms spilled out of an open doorway. She scrambled back to where the passageways intersected and tucked her body behind a slim column jutting out from the wall. The figures faced away from her, but Jessica recognized the black shields of the BorCron guards. Their dark forms faded down the passageway in the opposite direction; she expelled a long breath not realizing she had been holding it.

Cautiously, moving from the column's protection, Jessica approached the illuminated doorway. Removing the knives from her belt, she eased closer. Listening, barely breathing, her back flat to the wall, she peered around the door. No movement. Grasping a knife in each hand, she swung into the room, her body bent low, ready for confrontation. The room was empty. The familiar smell of food wafted over her senses. Hunger propelled her across the floor to a table strewn with bits and pieces of discarded meat and bread. Scooping up the remnants of what must have been the BorCrons' meal, she shoveled them into her mouth. *Water.* Jessica's eyes scanned the room. On a shelf to her right stood an aluminum water keg. Not bothering to look for a cup she pressed her parched lips to the spout and turned the handle. Cool water spilled over her lips and chin, cascading down the front of her jacket. Jessica drank deeply, each swallow a joy. When she'd had her fill she closed off the spout and wiped her mouth with the back of her hand.

The room was windowless with large aluminum storage bins occupying most of the floor space. A visual and simulator stood against the far wall. Jessica searched through each bin looking for whatever she might be able to use. One contained thermo suits. She tried on several before finding one that fit. In the other bins she discovered backpacks, flares and food packets. Ripping open a couple of the food packets, she wolfed down their contents before shoving more into one of the backpacks. *Wonderful, at least I won't starve.* After filling a large flask with water from the keg, Jessica zipped up the thermo suit and adjusted the backpack. Knives held ready at her sides, she stepped through the airlock just as the alarm echoed down the corridor in short piercing blasts.

She had traveled only a few hundred feet when the lit passageway ended, emptying into a large chamber merging with three tunnels at the opposite end of the chamber. The air had become dense and chilled. She fished out one of the flares. *Now, what? The BorCrons must have gone down one of these tunnels ahead of me. But which one?* Jessica's mind raced. She had to make a decision fast. Without a wrist-com, whatever choice she made would be uncertain at best. She dare not hesitate much longer. The BorCrons were sure to be hot on her tail any moment. *Well,* she thought, *life's a gamble no matter how you slice it.* Decision made, she struck a flare and slipped into one of the tunnels.

***

Two guards were standing over Naal's body when Vantra rushed into the cell. In the background the alarm was still pulsating up and down the corridors. "You stupid fools, why are you standing here? Activate the tracers and go after her. And shut off that damned alarm!"

The two men saluted and quickly exited the room to join the others in the hunt. Vantra stared down at the corpse. Flushed with rage he kicked Naal's lifeless form. "She should have slit your throat, you worthless scum."

"Your Highness," a breathless voice interrupted Vantra's furious onslaught. "The gravity tube has been activated. Three life forms are on their way into the caves."

"Then destroy them!" Vantra roared. "Must I do all your thinking for you?"

"Yes...I mean...no," stuttered the guard, fearing for his life. Saluting he quickly backed out of the room.

Vantra, hands balled into fists, swore into the air. "There's no way out, Calder, my BorCrons will find you. As for your would-be rescuers, they'll be as dead as this rotting carcass..." Vantra spat on Naal as he passed, his robe brushing across the dead man's face.

Chapter 15
Disaster

The gravity tube rocketed along a railed glass-enclosed path deep inside the caves, the pathway illuminated by lighting carved into the walls. Oxygen was fed into the caves by generators left running after the miners had abandoned the crystal. Jeweled streams of dried crystal sparkled along the dirt walls. The three men sat silent within the tube, each deep in his own thoughts.

Sweat trickled down Kraft's face as he shifted restlessly in his seat. His palms were damp with perspiration. Suddenly he began clawing at the harness holding him secure against the seat. Waving his arms like a mad man, he screamed, "I know what you're doing, you can't get rid of me that easy. I'll kill you all!"

Jarod released his own harness and sprang up to restrain Kraft, but he was too late. Kraft flung himself out of his seat and made a dash for the airlock, raving as though he were pursued by demons. Quad, who had leapt from his seat to intercept Kraft, made a grab for him just as the airlock opened. Suddenly a bone-jarring jolt shook the gravity tube.

Steel rods erupted through the center aisle spewing forth rocks in their wake. Several seats, nearest to the aisle, were ripped from their anchors and became airborne. Breaking glass whirled about the tube; a large piece slicing through the seat Kraft had just vacated. The tube was propelled off its tracks in a spray of dirt and rocks, friction igniting a fire beneath its undercarriage. Kraft was sent spiraling out into space, hands and feet clawing at air as the ear splitting noise of the derailed tube drowned his terrified cries. Quad and Jarod were tossed end over end across the seats and dropped in a heap as the tube settled in a mangled wreck several hundred feet down the tunnel.

Jarod groaned as he struggled to pull himself upright. He was wedged beneath two seats, which had collapsed on top of him. He tried to move but his left arm was pinned under him. A strangled moan sounded to his left. He could just make out Quad's form in the diminished light of the tube. "Quad...Quad, can you hear me?" A hazy smoke began curling its way through the wreckage. Jarod pushed harder against the seats, but they refused to budge. "The tube's on fire!" he shouted.

"I think my shoulder's dislocated," Quad groaned.

"Can you move?" Jarod asked.

Quad managed to rise to his good elbow. "Yeah, what about you?"

"I'm pinned under some seats but I don't think anything's broken. Do you think you can lift them off me?"

Quad struggled to his feet, his right arm dangling loosely at his side. He slowly stepped over the tangled mess and painfully made his way to where Jarod lay pinned. He gripped one of the seats in the crook of his good arm and lifted, gritting his teeth against the pain in his shoulder.

"It's not moving," Jarod coughed. "Try again!"

Quad gathered his strength, the veins in his neck protruding sharply as he poured all he had into the effort. A spasm of coughing over took him, bending him double, as smoke seared his lungs.

"Once more, Quad, I felt it give."

Quad struggled for breath, then gripped the seat and lifted with every ounce of strength that was left in him. It was enough. Jarod broke free. Coughing again and again, he staggered to his feet. "Com'on, we've gotta get out of here!"

The smoke lay thick as both men, choking, moved as one using the piled mass of overturned seats for support. The tube lay on its side at an angle, the airlock blocked with debris. A gaping hole had been ripped in the tube's side, wreckage was strewn everywhere. Jarod struggled to help Quad over the debris into the opening. He felt as though his lungs were being squeezed shut, acrid smoke burned his eyes impairing his vision. Quad stumbled and fell landing on his bad arm. He bit deep into his lower lip, biting back the jarring pain that seared along his neck and shoulder. Jarod grabbed hold of his suit and pulled him through the opening to the outside of the tube. They tumbled to the ground with a thud.

Jarod lay gasping for air, he felt bruised all over; Quad lay close by. Both men were bleeding; their face and hands cut by flying glass. Jarod crawled to the big man's side checking for a pulse, but then remembered Quad was a Borkian. "Dammit, Quad, I'm not sure where your pulse is!"

Quad rolled onto his side in a seizure of coughing. He spit out smoke and sucked in deep breaths of air. "God, I thought I was dead," he said, gritting his teeth against the pain in his shoulder.

"That's got to be reset," Jarod said, getting to his feet. He peeled off his thermo suit and removed his shirt from underneath, ripping it into strips. "These should keep your arm stable." Aiding the big man to his feet, he helped him remove his suit. Gripping Quad's injured arm, Jarod braced it with his own. He pressed the palm of his free hand flat against Quad's shoulder and steadied himself. "Ready?"

"Get on with it!" Quad said between clenched teeth.

Jarod gave a sharp tug, pressing into the joint at the same time. The shoulder snapped into place. Quad let out a loud grunt and let fly several Borkian oaths.

"That should do it," Jarod said. "Better keep it immobile, though, for the time being." He used the shirt strips to bind Quad's arm close to his chest, then helped him back into his suit, leaving the bound arm inside and the empty sleeve tucked into his suit belt. "If we had the Med-Pac I could give you something to ease the pain."

"Well we don't, so this will have to do," Quad said gruffly. "What the hell happened anyway?"

"I don't know..." Jarod answered thoughtfully. "The BorCron Directive said the tube was checked on a regular basis. Maybe someone doesn't like the idea of our being here."

"Well, they sure as hell knew how to get their point across," Quad countered.

"I'm worried about Kraft," Jarod said. "He could be lying back there hurt or dead for all we know. Are you up to walking?"

Quad ignored the question. "If that friend of yours hadn't freaked out...!"

"Wait a minute," Jarod cut in, "are you implying this was his fault?"

"I'm not implying anything, the man's been nothing but trouble."

Jarod, gray eyes intent, struggled to keep his anger under control. "Get one thing straight, Quad, I've known Kraft a hell of a lot longer than I've known you. I don't have to defend him to anyone, but just so you know where I stand, I'm not leaving these caves till I find him, and if you don't like the idea you can make your way back to the barracks and head back to New Earth for all I care."

Quad was fuming, his eyes blazing. "You forget, Jarod, we're here to find Jessica Caldar and by damn I'll do it with or without you!"

"Then do it without me!"

Jarod stalked off without a backward glance.

"Of all the damned fools," Quad said, glaring at Jarod's retreating back.

Chapter 16
Lost

The alarm had ceased and Jessica knew Vantra's guards probably weren't far behind. Her only hope was that she had chosen the right tunnel. Maybe they weren't familiar with all the tunnels and would search the others first; but then again...? Well, she couldn't dwell on that scenario she had to keep moving. The flare lit her way through a tangle of intersecting tunnels that seemed to go on forever. The food and water had restored most of her strength, but she soon grew weary and slumped to the ground resting her back against a rock, fatigue taking its toll. Her head bobbed several times before she drifted into a restless sleep.

He was there again waiting to take her hand, his face veiled in the mist as before, but this time Vantra stood between them blocking her way. Tears streamed down her cheeks leaving a dark stain. Then the man from the hovertrain appeared, brushing Vantra aside. Her way was clear now. She stepped forward to place her hand in the stranger's, but he turned and moved away. Don't go, please, don't go, I need you, I...need...you...

Jessica awoke, her cheeks damp with salty tears. She touched the wetness with her fingertip. *Why do I keep dreaming of this man? If only I could see his face, I might know what all this means.*

The temperature had dropped while she slept. Her breath was vaporizing and a cold chill settled on her face and hands. Removing gloves from an inside pocket, she slipped them over her fingers then struck another flare.

The tunnel merged into a large chamber. Jessica lifted the flare high above her head. Light reflected off the walls like jeweled prisms. *Must be one of the mining sites,* she thought. Droning, like that of an insect, brought her to full alert. The sound was coming along the tunnel she had just exited and was growing in intensity. She whipped her head from side to side searching for a place to hide. Spotting an outcrop of boulders to her left, she dove behind them extinguishing the flare just as two tracers flashed into view. Beams of light emitted from their small spiked bodies as they moved back and forth in mid air, while cameras imbedded in their metal frames transmitted pictures back to the main computer. Jessica knew they had the capability of firing stun-lasers to render their prey helpless.

She wedged her body tighter into the crevice of the rock. Though the tracers were fast, they still needed their camera eye to detect movement. If she stayed put she might have a chance. The tracers continued rotating, searching.

A low growl rumbled above her. She dared not look up; the movement would alert the tracers. Her flesh tingled; waiting was agony, knowing for certain that whatever was up there was signaling its intention to strike. The air prickled and fizzed as flashes split the darkness. The tracers had caught the creature's movement and fired. A screech pierced the air as the thing dropped within feet of Jessica's hiding place. The tracers whipped to the body, threads of light blinking on and off as they transmitted pictures of their prey back to the main computer. Jessica watched transfixed as the creature's eyes glowed red, then dimmed, as its life form was drained. The gray body jerked twice, then lay still.

As if sensing her presence the tracers whirled in unison. Jessica ceased breathing. For a moment they hovered over their prey, their thin trail of laser light rotating over the boulders. Then suddenly they darted away back down the tunnel, their droning fading into the darkness. Jessica couldn't believe her luck. She was certain they had discovered her, but the boulders must have concealed her better than she realized. Waiting, listening, for what seemed an eternity, she lit another flare.

The body of a gray tunnel feeder lay nearby. Jessica approached cautiously and knelt to examine the creature. The stun lasers, meant for larger prey, had been too powerful for the rat, killing it instead. It was huge, with fangs large enough to take off a man's hand. Jessica shuddered, wondering how many more were roaming the tunnels. Her hand automatically slid to her belt. The laser and holster were gone, but she still had the two knives taken from Naal's body. *They'll have to do,* she thought, rising to her feet. Taking one last look at the dead feeder, Jessica retrieved her backpack and continued her search along the walls of the chamber.

What little light the flare gave off the shadowy recesses of the cave seemed to devour. The air was stale with the odor of damp earth. The dull thud of her boots seemed to keep pace with the constantly dripping water seeping through the ceiling and walls. At times she thought she heard the clicking of clawed feet on stone. Her free hand never left the hilt of one of the knives.

As she neared the far end of the expanse the gurgle of water drew her attention. Lifting the flare higher, Jessica discovered a shallow stream. Scooping up a handful of water she tasted it on the tip of her tongue; it was cool and refreshing. She drank then filled her flask. Hoping the stream would lead her to an opening, she followed its flow.

Mist began to rise from the water's surface, as the stream grew wider and swifter. The chamber walls narrowed, forcing her to abandon the dry ground for the icy pool of water that surged around her, threatening to unbalance her as it shoved her forward. Holding the flare high above her head to keep it dry, she fought the current, struggling to stay upright.

A spur of land appeared ahead dividing the water into two separate channels. Shaking badly, teeth chattering, she pulled herself out onto the bank. Water had soaked the lower part of her body, but the backpack had remained dry. Shivering, she burrowed one end of the flare into the ground then pulled out a thermo canister from the backpack and broke the seal. Immediately heat radiated around her chilled body and began drying her clothes. Exhausted, she stretched out on her side next to the flare and drifted into a dreamless void.

The sound of swiftly moving water woke her. Confused at first by her surroundings, Jessica rolled onto her back and stared up at the dirt ceiling. *Oh, God, I'm still here in this hellhole!* Sitting up, she rested her chin on her knees and hugged her legs, her mind dwelling on the hopelessness of her situation. The short rest had helped her body, but uneasy thoughts raced through her mind, threatening bitter defeat. *If I don't make it out of here what will happen to you, Legend? I'm afraid.* A tear slipped from one eye marking a thin trail down her dirt-caked cheek as she thought of her friend and mentor.

She was brought up short knowing what his answer would be to this sad display of self-pity. Jessica angrily swept the tear aside with the back of her hand and flung back her head. Like an erupting volcano, words boiled to the surface and she yelled at the dirt ceiling, "No! I won't give up!"

Drawing strength from the vehemence of her own anger, she jumped to her feet, gathered up her things, and proceeded to follow the channel.

Chapter 17
Kell

Jarod limped past the debris left in the wake of the destroyed tube. He felt like hell and his legs stung as though licked by fire, but Kraft was his objective and nothing, including Quad, was going to keep him from finding his friend.

"Kraft, Kraft," his voice echoed through cupped hands. "Where are you?" The tunnel lights blinked as though mocking his efforts. *At least I'm not stumbling around in the dark*, he thought. His vid-com was useless; the weight that had pinned his arm had also crushed the communicator. Removing it from his wrist, he flung it aside.

The temperature had dropped considerably. He hadn't noticed the torn sections of his thermo suit before, with all that had happened, but now he could feel the cold seeping in through the holes. His gloves were with his gear scattered somewhere throughout the tangled mess that used to be a gravity tube. He pulled the thermo hood over his head and blew warm breath into his fisted hands. The vapor from his breath curled in a moist cloud as he thought back to another time his friend had been missing.

***

"Control, this is Jarod Krinner, any word from Commander Taybor?"

"No, sir, he's eight hours overdue. Space command has ordered two star-flyers dispatched. A severe electrical storm over Sector Three may have caused him to set down."

"Well notify me as soon as you have word."

"Yes, sir," the man replied, adding, "Commander Taybor is an excellent pilot, sir, he can take care of himself."

When control center blinked off Jarod banged the desk with his fist. "He'd better or I'll wring his damn neck!"

"Hey, ole buddy, I hear you've been worried about me." Kraft's wide grin filled Jarod's screen several hours later.

Jarod leaned back in his chair and crossed his ankles on the desktop, looking for all the world like a man who could care less. It had been twelve hours since Kraft's flyer had disappeared. "What makes you think I was worried?" Jarod quipped, turning from the screen and picking up a sheet of paper to study its content.

"I'd say for one thing, base command said you were driving them nuts, and for another I know you too well. Come on admit it. You thought your best friend was a goner." Kraft puckered his lips as though to kiss the screen.

"Get that ugly face off my screen," Jarod snapped, unable to keep from smiling.

Kraft laughed. "OK, buddy, but then I won't be able to tell you what happened, and you won't sleep tonight for wanting to know all the details."

"What details?" Jarod asked, taking his feet off the desk and leaning toward the screen.

"I knew that would get your attention," Kraft laughed.

Jarod stood and crossed his arms. "You know, Kraft, you can be a real pain in the ass."

"I know, but I'm the best pain in the ass you've got."

Jarod burst into laughter. "Okay, hot-shot, let's hear it. What stunt did you pull this time to get yourself on the missing roster?"

Kraft looked hurt. "Now what makes you think I'd do anything out of the ordinary? Sorry to disappoint you, pal, but this time my flyer got hit by an electrical storm and knocked out my readings. I had to make an emergency landing and sit tight till someone decided I was worth searching for. I'm returning to retrieve my flyer as soon as I can get into the area. Not about to lose a jewel like her. But right now I'm due for a shower and some shuteye. Talk to you later." Kraft signed off.

Jarod sat for a few minutes staring at the blank screen, his expression one of relief that his friend was safe and back on base.

***

But this time it was not an electrical storm. "Damn fool," Jarod muttered aloud. "Where the hell are you?" His words were becoming slurred. "Don't know how much longer I can go on...getting tired..." The temptation to drop to the ground and rest was growing stronger, but in this cold he knew if he fell asleep he might not wake up, and he had to stay lucid. Using the dirt wall for support, he kept up a slow, dragging pace, calling out Kraft's name. A shadow of movement alerted him; squinting, he called out, "Kraft, is that you?"

A disheveled and wild-eyed Kraft yelled back at him, "Don't come any closer!" His hand was outstretched to ward off Jarod's advance, in the other he held a laser. Blood dripped from a gash in his cheek.

"Hey it's me, pal," Jarod said gently, moving cautiously towards his friend. He figured Kraft was hallucinating because of the feeder's poisonous bite; he had to get help for his friend soon or he would die. Jarod moved closer.

"I warn you, I'll kill you," Kraft yelled, his face a mask of fear, sweat streaming from his pores. He raised the laser and fired. Jarod hurled himself to the side as the beam grazed his shoulder, ripping open his thermo suit. Kraft fired again, but missed; dirt flew through the air as the beam split off a section of wall behind Jarod. Panicking, Kraft turned and fled, his crazed cries fading away down the tunnel.

Jarod staggered to his feet and held his arm. He didn't think the cut went deep, but thank God, Kraft was a lousy shot. Still, he was dangerous considering his condition. *I've got to get you back to base, old friend, but how the hell am I gonna do that? First I've got to find you. Damn, you're not making it easy!*

Cold was seeping into his bones and sleep was not far behind. Jarod knew he couldn't continue this fruitless search. He had to find shelter soon or die from the cold. He started back the way he had come, hoping at least Quad was mobile. Maybe one of them could reach the cruiser and go for help.

A dark figure stepped from the shadows.

Jarod narrowed his eyes to bring the figure into focus. "Kraft, thank God. I knew..." The words died on his lips. The man was nothing like Kraft. He was tall and angular; clean-shaven with silver hair cropped close to his head, and he was dressed completely in black. Jarod shook his head. "What the...?"

"Don't be alarmed, Jarod, I've come to help." The voice was smooth, yet held a note of authority. As Jarod drew near, he found himself staring into a pair of startling blue eyes.

"I'm not alarmed, just curious. Who are you? And how is it you know my name?"

"My name is Kell. That's all you need to know for now. We've plenty of time to talk later. Come."

Jarod staggered slightly, but straightened. "I'm not going with you or anyone else until I find my friend."

"He will be fine. My people will find him and take him to Sanctuary. Right now I need to get you to shelter. Come, I have warmth waiting for you."

Jarod eyed Kell with suspicion. "Why aren't you wearing cold weather gear? It's freezing in these caves."

Kell ignored the question. Moving to the rock wall, he pressed his hand into an indentation surrounded by alien symbols. The wall rippled in rings, as when pebbles are tossed into a lake, and opened before them. Kell motioned Jarod through.

Warmth and light radiated from a sphere positioned in the middle of a crystal-lined room. Marble benches encircled the sphere. "Sit and warm yourself," Kell said, pointing to one of the benches. "You must be hungry." Kell moved to the far end of the room and returned with a basket of fresh fruit.

"Where did you get these?" Jarod questioned, lifting a pear from the basket. "The only place I've ever seen such fruit is in the archives. They don't exist any more."

"Please, taste," Kell encouraged, sitting alongside Jarod. "They are real, I assure you."

Jarod studied Kell in the light. Pale skin, drawn tight over angular features, appeared almost translucent. His fingers were longer than those of a human, and the eyes! A fiery metallic blue. Kell did not appear to be New Earthian.

Sweeping the basket aside, Jarod sprang to his feet and stood over the man. Who are you, and where are you planning to take Kraft? If you harm him...!"

Kell answered evenly, "Your friend, Kraft, and the Borkian, Quad, will be taken to Sanctuary and well cared for. However, Chaser Caldar is another matter; she is still missing. We must find her soon; time is running out."

"So Caldar *is* here?" Jarod said. Eyes narrowed he asked suspiciously, "How is it you know so much about what's happening?"

Kell raised his hand and nodded. "I understand your frustration, Jarod, but there is no time to explain everything." As though appeasing a petulant child, Kell continued. "I promise, your questions will be answered when we reach Sanctuary, but now we must find Jessica." Reaching beneath the sphere, Kell removed two small objects and handed them to Jarod. "Place these inside your jacket, the sphere will continue to energize the crystals and keep you warm."

Jarod realized it was futile to continue questioning Kell. He would just have to wait until they reached Sanctuary, what or wherever that was. He slipped the crystals into an inner pocket of his jacket and immediately felt warmth radiate through his body. Turning to Kell, he warned, "Kraft had better be in good hands, as you said, or I'll tear the place apart."

Kell smiled. "There will be no need."

Chapter 18

Trapped

Time waned as though it no longer existed. Jessica's world had become an aching loneliness encasing her in a tomb of dirt, moving her farther from reality. The river had spilled into an underground waterway sometime back leaving her no way to follow its path. She was continually fighting the urge to give up. Even her sight began playing tricks on her. Several times she thought she found openings only to discover they were distortions in the dirt walls.

The tunnel she had been following merged into a large cave. Raising the flare overhead, she noticed a line of ledges running high along the walls then dipping down to ground level. About a dozen holes were bored into the hard surface above the ledges. She was looking up when her foot slipped on a loose stone jarring her off balance. The flare fell from her grasp and dropped to the ground spitting out white sparks as it rolled away from her. Jessica made a dive for the flare landing hard on her stomach, but before she could grab it, the flare vanished from sight and she found herself staring over the edge of an abyss. Pulling back in alarm, she watched as the flare tumbled end over end out of sight, its thuds echoing off the walls.

"God, that could have been me!" Her voice was trembling.

Lying still for a moment to regain her composure, she slowly removed the backpack from her shoulders, then turned onto her back and felt inside for another flare; only three remained. *I may die in this hellhole, but I'll be damned if I'm going to do it in the dark.* Shifting from her back, she boosted herself to a sitting position and removed a thermo canister from the backpack, along with a packet of food.

A slight sound alerted her. Tense, she listened, squinting into the darkness beyond the limited light of the flare and canister, but the sound wasn't repeated. *Probably some shifting dirt,* she thought, easing back against the backpack. *But then…*Removing the two knives taken from Naal's body she tucked them securely at her sides.

Unconsciously she touched the cut at her temple. Her thoughts flashed back to what Protendel had said just before his knife pierced her skin. "I won't be *their* errand boy." Vantra and Naal, that's who he meant, she was sure of it, but she was still at a loss as to what they wanted with her, or how her father was involved? Naal had murdered her father, but Vantra was the real culprit. *I'll avenge your death, Father, even if I have to kill Vantra myself.*

Soft shadows from the canister's light caressed her lovely features as her thoughts drifted back in time. She had been born on New Earth to parents who valued life and honesty. Both were gone now, but Jessica had inherited their values. At the age of ten she had adamantly informed her father, "I want to become a Chaser and put Evaders in prison."

He had smiled down at her caressing her cheek with his hand. "And a wonderful one you'll make too, when the time comes."

The desire never left as she grew to womanhood. Over the years, encouraged by her father's faith in her, she had worked harder than ever to achieve her goal. At seventeen she was accepted as a cadet into the Federation. Her father sat with tears of pride when she was promoted to Chaser a year ahead of her fellow cadets.

"You need a social life, Jessica," he used to scold. "You've got to do something besides hunt criminals and take care of a dull old man."

She had wrapped her arms around her father and planted a kiss on top of his head. "I'll have plenty of time for that later, Father, right now you're the only man I want in my life. And you're anything but dull."

She never had the social life her father had wanted for her. His death had thrown her deeper into her work and she didn't have time for men. Legend was her companion and friend; all she needed, so she thought at that moment. But moments grew into months, and months into years and she was still alone.

***

One by one, gray forms emerged from nests high overhead and moved stealthily along the dirt ledges to ground level. They signaled one another with low rumblings as they advanced towards the still form outlined in shadow. The group held back as one of the rats moved in closer sniffing the air, its lips curled back over curved fangs.

Jessica stiffened sensing the predator's presence. Slowly her fingers curled around the knife handles. From the low rumblings she judged there to be several. Her heart was pounding and her hands felt clammy. She needed to keep her wits about her; if she made a move they would strike in force.

She breathed deeply and waited. The rat crept forward, nose high in the air, sniffing, its eyes a red glow in the muted light. Then picking up her scent it screeched wildly and sprang. Gripping the knives in both hands, Jessica slashed upward, at the same time rolling sideways away from the feeder's gnashing fangs. The animal writhed in pain, its throat sliced clean through, greenish fluid oozing from the gaping wounds. The others, ignoring Jessica, pounced on the helpless feeder threshing in agony, cannibalizing it.

Jessica jumped to her feet but before she had a chance to escape two feeders broke from the pack and blocked her way, their fangs bared, dripping green fluid. They were even bigger than the one the tracers had killed. She backed away slowly sliding one foot behind the other, knives clutched in her fisted hands. The feeders rumbled an alarm. Leaving their meal, the others turned, moving as one they slowly edged their way towards Jessica, their red eyes blazing. As they charged in for the kill, Jessica jerked backwards to avoid their slashing fangs and stepped out into the void. She screamed as her body plummeted into the dark abyss.

Chapter 19

Rescue

As they exited the crystal room, Kell handed Jarod a flashlight and an oblong object. "Keep your eye on the readings. They will help us in our search for Chaser Caldar."

Jarod turned to face Kell squarely, his expression hard. "This is a DNA activated tracer. How the hell did you get you hands on Caldar's DNA? Only the Federation has that information!" His eyes bore into Kell's. "Straight answers, Kell, no more of this runaround you've been giving me!"

Kell's eyes glowed a brilliant blue, freezing Jarod to the spot. "Now," he addressed Jarod's still form, removing the tracer from his hand, "I believe we shall continue this conversation later." He downloaded Jessica's DNA signature into the vortex of his brain and concealed the tracer beneath his coat. Fixing his gaze once more on Jarod's placid face, he released him from the trance.

Jarod shook his head. He couldn't remember what Kell had said. "What?"

"I said we'll follow this tunnel for a while."

Jarod hesitated, feeling lightheaded.

"Are you all right?" Kell asked solicitously.

"Yes, why shouldn't I be?" Jarod responded brusquely. "Let's go."

Kell took the lead, his computerized brain secretly picking up Jessica's signature as they trekked through several tunnels and caves. Jarod thought the man was never going to rest. When they came to a slow moving stream Jarod dropped to his knees and dipped his cupped hands into the water bringing it to his lips. Kell stood at the water's edge staring straight ahead. "Aren't you thirsty?" Jarod asked.

"I believe we'll have to wade," Kell said, ignoring the question as he stepped into the water.

Jarod moved to Kell's side. The water soaked through his boots sending a chill up his legs. "Look, we've been traveling for miles in this dirt hole, what makes you so sure we're going in the right direction?"

"You'll just have to trust me," Kell replied. "I believe we are close."

Jarod frowned. "I haven't seen a thing to indicate Caldar came this way other than that dead tunnel feeder, and who's to say she killed the thing?"

"You have much to learn, Jarod Krinner."

"What's that supposed to mean?"

Kell moved away. "Come, we haven't time to debate."

Jarod grabbed Kell's arm and swung him around creating a small swell in the water. "You mean *you* don't have time to debate!" he snapped. His temper was riding on a short fuse and he'd had just about enough of Kell and his smug self-assurance.

Kell sighed patiently lifting Jarod's fingers from his arm. "I promise you, when we find Jessica you will have your answers."

"You mean, *if*, we find Caldar."

"For a man as dedicated as you, Jarod, I would think you might have more faith."

"My faith is not at question here. You are."

"Fair enough." Kell strode off upstream leaving a seething Jarod to follow. *He's as stubborn as Quad and Kraft put together.*

They reached a strip of dry land and climbed out onto the bank. Jarod flashed his light over the soft ground. Motioning to Kell he pointed to an indentation in the dirt. He bent and picked up the lid of a thermo canister examining it. "One thing's for sure, someone camped here."

"We must continue," Kell said urgently. He paused and raised his hand. "Listen."

"What is it?" Jarod asked, moving to Kell's side.

"I'm not sure." Kell stood motionless, intent, staring ahead. "Quick," he said, bursting into a run, "Jessica's in danger!"

"How the hell do you..." Before Jarod could finish his sentence a scream echoed down the tunnel ahead of them. They rushed into a large cave just in time to see Jessica tumble out of sight. A dozen tunnel rats were crouched low to the ground clawing at the chasm's edge, screeching in rage at the loss of their prey. Hearing the men, they whirled around, fangs snapping and eyes aflame with fury. As one they crept forward intending to circle their new victims. Kell shouted over his shoulder at Jarod, "Stand back!" and advanced towards the rats.

"For God's sake, Kell, those things will tear you to pieces!"

Red-hot streaks of light flashed from Kell's fingers as he raised them towards the circling rats. A high-pitched whine mingled with that of the feeder's screeches as their gray bodies were reduced to black ash. The few that remained scattered and fled up the ledges disappearing into their nests high overhead.

Jarod stared at Kell. He started to speak, but Kell cut him short. "Hurry, see what you can do for Caldar."

Jarod rushed to the spot where they had seen her go over. He heard a groan. "She's still alive," he shouted back at Kell. Flashlight in hand, he slipped to his stomach and peered over the edge of the chasm. Humid billowing vapors rose from its depths. Kell moved to Jarod's prone figure.

"She's lying on a ledge some ten feet below," Jarod said, looking up at Kell. "And from what I can see I don't think it's going to hold much longer."

"You have to bring her up," Kell stated matter-of-factly.

"And how do you propose I do that?" Jarod responded angrily. "Short of sprouting wings, I have no way of reaching her!"

Kell pulled a thin line from his belt. "Here, use this."

Jarod flashed the beam of his flashlight around the cave. Frustrated, he replied, "There's nothing to anchor it to."

"Yes there is. Me. Trust me, Jarod."

"I suppose I have no choice. I never thought I'd put my life in the hands of an Android, but that little episode with the lasers gave you away. You might have let me know sooner. Or were you afraid I'd kill you?"

Kell ignored the question.

"Okay, let's get this over with," Jarod said, knowing from experience he wasn't going to get an answer.

Tucking the flashlight into his thermo suit to free his hands, he wrapped the line around his waist and held on as Kell lowered him over the edge letting the line out slowly. Jessica lay face down on a narrow ledge. He signaled Kell to let out more line so that he was level with her body. Jessica groaned and lifted her head.

"Can you move?" he asked.

"I think so," she replied weakly, shifting to her side. "I don't think anything's broken."

"Good, I'm going to get as close as I can. Try to put your arms around my neck."

Jessica pulled herself up just as a piece of ledge broke away and dropped out of sight. "It's giving way," she gasped.

Jarod swung in closer and reached for her. "Quick take my hand."

Jessica screamed as the ledge split and crumbled beneath her. Jarod made a wild grab for her wrist. "I've got you!"

They were swinging wildly over the chasm; the beam of Jarod's flashlight making crazily circles over the walls. "Try to reach my arm with your other hand," he yelled down at her.

The dirt wall that had held the ledge began crumbling away cascading into the chasm, releasing choking dust into the air.

"Pull us up," Jarod shouted at Kell, coughing hard as dust seared his lungs. "I can't hold on much longer!" His grip was slipping. Jessica's struggle to grab his arm with her free hand was putting pressure on his hold and his fingers were losing strength. She felt her wrist sliding through his hand; with one last effort she swung her body up and grabbed for his arm. Pain seared through Jarod's injured shoulder as she connected and he gritted his teeth. Fighting for breath, Jessica held on for dear life and looked up into the face of her rescuer.

Jarod coughed and grimaced, "Well done."

Kell pulled them to the surface and released the line from Jarod's waist. He pressed a small indention in his belt allowing the line to slip back into place then stepped into the shadows.

They lay coughing, struggling to catch their breath. Finally Jarod stood shakily to his feet and offered Jessica his hand. "Are you hurt?"

She let him pull her to her feet; they were standing only

inches apart. "No, but if you hadn't come along when you did..."

He was looking into the depths of two very green eyes. "Ah yes...well," he stuttered. She was conscious of his nearness.

"You're shivering," he said.

"Am I?" she answered, suddenly aware that she was.

"You're thermo suit is torn. It must have happened in the fall. Here, this will keep you warm." Reaching into his suit, he extracted one of the crystals.

"What's this?" she questioned.

"Hard to explain right now, just put it close to your body."

Jessica accepted the crystal without further questions and did as instructed. The chill dissipated immediately.

"I could have died down there if you hadn't come when you did. How..." She broke off, her brows knitted together in a suspicious frown. "Or are you one of Vantra's mercenaries?" Backing away, her eyes searched for the knives she had dropped, her voice turned frosty. "In that case I'd have to kill you."

Jarod held up his hands as though to ward her off. "Whoa," he chuckled, closing the gap she had created between them until they were almost touching. "I have yet to hear a thanks." He looked amused. "Oh, but I forgot I was planning to kill you so guess that doesn't count."

His eyes dropped to her neck; his senses throbbed in rhythm to the pulse of her throat and her heaving chest. Stepping back to widen the space between them, he asked seriously, "Why the hell should Prince Vantra send mercenaries after you? I thought your assignment was to find *him*?" This snip of a woman was getting to him and he resented her accusation, especially after he had risked his own neck to save hers. This time his voice was gruff.

"If I were a mercenary, you'd be at the bottom of that

chasm now." Turning on his heels, he shouted over his shoulder, "If you must thank someone for rescuing your thankless hide you can thank Kell!"

"Of all the...!" Jessica stormed after him stepping into his path, her lips compressed in anger. "If you're not with Vantra then who the hell are you? And who is this...this, Kell?" She was so angry she was stuttering. The man was infuriating.

Jarod stood his ground. "He's the Android who destroyed the tunnel feeders that were ready to make a meal of you, and hauled us up out of that pit, which, I might add, kept that pretty face of yours from being smashed to a bloody pulp. I'm a Chaser like yourself. If you must know, my name is Jarod Krinner."

"Oh..." Jessica said haltingly, the fight going out of her as she stared wide-eyed into his angry face. "I was supposed to meet you at command headquarters. How...?"

"How did I get here?" Jarod finished for her. "It's a long story; suffice it to say you were reported missing so we came looking for you."

Jessica looked around. "We? I suppose you mean this Kell, whoever he is?"

Before Jarod could explain that he meant Kraft and Quad, Kell, having observed the angry exchange between the two with amusement, stepped into view. "I believe he means me," he said evenly, turning on his flashlight.

Jessica looked surprised. You!"

"You know him?" Jarod asked, puzzled.

"Only from a Federation file," she said, her eyes narrowing in suspicion. "He was being shoved into a hovertrain at the time. But his appearance was quite different then."

Kell smiled mysteriously and placed an arm across his chest, bowing slightly. "I believe you are speaking of the Eternians capture ten years ago. I'm surprised you recognized me."

Jarod looked from one to the other. "What's this all about?"
Kell sighed, "Always the questions."

"And I'll continue to ask them till you give me some answers!" he snapped.

"I'd like a few myself," Jessica said. "Just what is your connection with the Eternians?" She recalled her mission, to locate him and discover if he, or the Eternians, had anything to do with Prince Vantra's disappearance. Obviously, since Vantra was not missing but playing some kind of mind game, with her as the bait, Kell must be another part of the puzzle.

"I assure you both I am not your enemy, quite the contrary."

"You keep saying that," Jarod flared.

"Enough of this, we're wasting time. Come!" Kell walked away leaving them to follow.

Jarod turned to Jessica who hesitated. "Well?"

"I believe you're the one holding the flashlight; I don't think I have much choice," she said irritably.

"Suit yourself," he said, turning away.

As Jessica stooped to retrieve her backpack a wave of dizziness swept over her. She swayed slightly as she lifted it to her shoulders.

Kell moved swiftly along the passageways he and Jarod had taken in their search for Jessica. But she was still weak from her ordeal over the past two days and was lagging farther behind. She stumbled a couple of times but refused to give in and ask Kell or Jarod to slow their pace.

"He must have night vision," Jarod mumbled aloud. Hearing no reply from Jessica, he turned to see if she was keeping up. *Probably wishing she had a knife to stab me in the back with.* But she wasn't behind him. He pointed the beam back down the tunnel where she lay in a heap, her slumped body braced against a boulder.

"Kell," he shouted through cupped hands. "Hold up,

Caldar's collapsed." He moved to her side and gathered her in his arms, lifting her chin with his hand. *A beautiful face,* he thought. *Too bad she doesn't have the temperament to match.* She moaned and Jarod leaned closer, their lips almost touching.

Kell stood over them, a sly grin marking his otherwise placid features.

"I was checking to see if she was breathing." *Damnit,* he thought, *why do you need to explain yourself to an Android?*

Before Jarod could object, Kell bent and swept Jessica's limp body up into his arms. "We're almost there."

Jessica came to, dazed and indignant. "Put me down, I can walk!"

Kell ignored her protests and moved quickly along the tunnel. She caught a glimpse of Jarod over the Android's shoulder. He seemed to be enjoying her predicament. She hammered on Kell. "Put me down, you walking computer!"

"I don't think he's listening," Jarod chuckled.

"Mind your own damn business!" Jessica threw at him, frustrated that he was witnessing her humiliation.

Kell entered a short passageway and pressed his hand to the wall. As before, when they entered the sphere room, an opening appeared and Kell stepped through with Jessica in his arms. Following close behind, Jarod heard a sharp intake of breath from Jessica as Kell lowered her to her feet. "Welcome to Sanctuary."

Chapter 20
Sanctuary

They stood beneath a huge domed ceiling. Before them, an edifice shining as pure crystal rose from the midst of a blue reflecting pool. A wide bridge spanned the pool and ended beneath a high archway surrounded by alien symbols. Beams radiated from the top of the structure and moved along the dome creating warmth and light. Facets of color reflected the beauty of green lawns and multicolored flowers growing in profusion. Clipped hedges lined the walkways encircling the building, culminating at the archway.

"You may remove your thermo suits," Kell said. "I believe you will find the temperature quite comfortable."

As she and Jarod slipped out of their suits Jessica dropped to one knee. Head bent, she ran a hand over the soft grass. "It's not artificial," she exclaimed, looking up at Kell with wonderment. "What is this place?"

"A new beginning you might say," he replied. "Come, your arrival has been anticipated for some time now." He turned to Jarod. "I believe there is someone you have been wanting to see."

As he was talking, several men and women in white robes excitedly exited the building and crossed the bridge towards them. A young woman stepped forward from the others.

"Myra," Kell said, addressing the small woman, "I believe Chaser Krinner is anxious to see his friend."

Myra turned and reached into the group of waiting people. The next thing Jarod knew he was hauled off his feet by two crushing arms.

"It's about time you got here, you sorry excuse of a friend." Kraft was grinning from ear to ear. He lowered Jarod's feet to the ground and turned to the woman at his side. "Myra, I want you to meet the best damn friend a man ever had. Give him a big kiss. If you don't, I will."

Jarod laughed. "I think I'd prefer, Myra, thanks." He held Kraft at arm's length. "How the hell did you get here? The last time I saw you, you were catapulted out of the tube, not to mention the raving lunatic you turned in to." Jarod looked hard at his friend. "You don't look any worse for wear."

Kraft grinned and pulled Myra close, wrapping an arm around her waist. "This little lady saved my life."

Myra stepped on tiptoes and kissed his cheek. "Not I. You know that." She hugged Kraft's arm and smiled up at Jarod. We're so glad you're safe."

Jarod frowned. "What about, Quad?"

"He's all right," Kraft answered. "Kell will fill you in on all that's happened."

"He's not exactly what I'd call free with information," Jarod said, eyeing Kell who stood conversing with the others.

"You'll get used to him," Kraft grinned. "He's really not so bad for a computer." He leaned into Jarod. "Remember I told you about my experience as a cadet aboard the Aurora bringing the Eternians to Pragora? It turns out Kell was the guy who revealed what the BorCrons looked like and how they were created from Vantra's cloned mistakes. It seems he's able to alter his appearance when needed. I didn't recognize him at first. Must be great to never age; could use some of that myself." Kraft smiled down at Myra and squeezed her waist.

Jarod lifted his hand to Kraft's shoulder and directed him and Myra to where Jessica stood. "Jessica Caldar, I'd like you to meet my friend, Commander Kraft Taybor." Then he nodded towards Myra. "And this is Myra."

Extending her hand first to Myra and then Kraft, Jessica smiled. "Commander."

Kraft covered her hand with his. "Hey, not so formal, just call me Kraft." He threw a meaningful glance at Jarod. "I understand you're the one Jarod here has been searching for?" Jarod glared at him. Kraft thought to himself, *Jarod, old boy, I think you've found your match. She's a beauty.*

Jessica swayed slightly; Myra caught the movement. "Oh, you men," she scolded, pushing Kraft aside, "standing around talking. Can't you see this young woman needs rest?"

Squinting at Jessica, she said, "And from the looks of it a little food wouldn't hurt either. Come with me, Jessica, we'll leave these insensitive brutes to themselves." Before Jessica could protest, Myra tucked her arm through hers and marched her over the bridge into a room filled with glowing candles, quiet music and soft furniture. She ushered Jessica to a large chair near two potted plants covered in brilliant foliage. Opposite the chair, sitting on a low table, stood a huge vase alive with yellow and orange blooms. Myra's voice was gentle when she spoke. "There now, sit and rest I'll bring you something to eat."

Jessica's battered and weary body melted into the comfortable chair. The fragrance of flowers wafted around her, filling her senses with a calmness she rarely felt. She fought the urge to sleep but her eyelids slowly closed.

When Myra returned she smiled down at Jessica's sleeping form and laid aside the food-laden tray. Reaching into the folds of her gown she extracted a small oval stone. Its smooth surface glowed in the palm of her hand as she passed it along Jessica's body. The cuts and bruises Jessica had sustained as a result of her capture began to disappear, and her skin took on a healthy glow. Even the scar from Protandel's knife faded, as though it had never been. Jessica sighed in her sleep. A faint smile creased the edges of her lips as her dreams transported her into another dimension.

Covering her with a blanket, Myra couldn't help wondering what part this quiet beauty held in the Ancients plans for Jarod Krinner? *Is she the one destined to be with him to enter Eterna?* Myra sighed and thought, *Vantra's evil is a black hole sucking everything into its nucleus.*

***

An elderly man in flowing white robe approached Kell and the others as they conversed with the people of Sanctuary. The small gathering parted and lowered their heads in respect when he greeted them.

He addressed Kell first. "I see you have found our friend." He turned and smiled at Jarod. "Welcome to Sanctuary."

The man was thin and wrinkled; his face ancient and mystical.

"Jarod," Kell began introductions, "this is Elgron Razzune, guardian of Eterna and keeper of the PROPHECY."

Razzune placed a hand on Jarod's good shoulder. His eyes were keen and clear. "We have waited a long time for this day, Jarod Krinner. Or should I address you by your proper name, Jarod Faus?"

"How…?" Jarod started to speak, but Razzune continued.

"Your grandfather was a great man and ruled New Earth with justice and peace. His death at the hands of that madman, Bardas Vantra, was a great loss. Our people have suffered much under *his* rule." Then Razzune's face brightened. "But now you are here; the Ancients have been informed and will make their appearance soon. In the meantime," he motioned to everyone, "come. Our friend here has had an arduous journey and must eat and rest."

As he led the group into the building Jarod was struck by the jeweled appearance of their surroundings. "It looks like crystal," he commented, "but I suspect there's more to it than that?"

"Yes," Razzune answered. "It is crystal fused with diamonds from the planet Alton-Gandorus; stronger than most metals, yet pliable to the workman's tools."

Crystal columns stood as majestic sentinels on each side of the great hall. The building seemed to radiate its own source of light and warmth. Alien symbols, similar to those opening the way into Sanctuary, stood out in profile along the walls. Razzune pointed to them.

"These are writings depicting the history of a race of people once called Trykonians." He paused. "However, they are known to you as the Ancients. It is they who built Sanctuary and have cared for us these past ten years."

He led Jarod to the center of the hall. Resting open on a luminous pedestal lay a large book, its pages covered in ancient script. A gentle breeze rustled the pages as though an invisible hand had turned them.

"The Prophecy is open to all who seek its wisdom," Razzune said. "It was given to us by the Ancients. In it is depicted the fulfillment of our people who will one day be rescued from a great disaster and given a planet of our own, called Eterna. Not only will we live in peace, but also the galaxy will follow suit. You see, Jarod, we Eternians have a great legacy to fulfill. Our future lies in the hands of the Ancients who have guided us for generations, but only a few have been privy to the knowledge. Eterna awaits those who have not fallen victim to Prince Vantra's evil.

"But come, let us tend to your wounds first, then we shall talk of things that are and things that are to be." He signaled Kell who moved ahead and opened a pair of tall-carved doors opening into a dining area.

"This is where we share our meals," Razzune said, pointing to a large slate table at its center. "Beyond are living quarters to accommodate those desiring to remain with us." He motioned to everyone. "Please, let us be seated."

Jarod sat to Razzune's left; Kraft and Myra occupied the seats across from Jarod.

"We shall eat soon," Razzune said, "but first we must tend to our friend's wounds." He whispered something into Kell's ear; Kell nodded and disappeared through a small doorway. Returning, bearing a beautifully carved box, he offered it to Razzune. "No, my friend, I think you should do the honors," he said.

Kell moved to Jarod's side and extracted a small stone from the box. He placed it in his palm and extended his hand towards Jarod. Jarod jumped to his feet and stayed Kell's hand with his own, holding it firm. "What the devil is that?" he asked suspiciously, glaring into Kell's unsettling blue eyes. The room fell into a placid silence as all the Eternians turned questioning eyes to Razzune.

He sighed and stood to his feet, placing a gentle hand on Jarod's shoulder. "Peace, my fiery one," he said softly, "it is called a healing stone. Though your wounds are not serious they are still in need of attention." He motioned to Kraft pleadingly. "Please, assure your friend we mean him no harm."

Kraft leaned across the table, his eyes boring into Jarod's. "You know I wouldn't lie to you. That tunnel feeder poison nearly killed me. I was a mess; out of my mind and ravin' mad, like I was being chased by hellfire itself. If it hadn't been for these good people I'd be a pile of quiverin' flesh fit only for space garbage." Kraft settled back in his chair and turned to Myra, cupping her chin in his hand. "This lovely little lady passed one of those stones over me and I'm good as new, even better." Turning back to Jarod, he said gruffly, "So sit down and let Kell do his job, or *keep* those scratches and burns and I hope they hurt like hell. By the way, I'm sorry about that," he said, looking sheepish, pointing to the spot where his laser had grazed Jarod's flesh.

Jarod rubbed his shoulder. "You always were a lousy shot."

Reluctantly he resumed his seat, glad that Caldar wasn't there to witness this exchange, although he didn't exactly know why he should care. Nodding hesitantly at the patiently waiting Kell, he snapped, "All right, but no funny stuff!"

The corners of Kraft's lips turned upward but he managed to maintain a sober expression as he watched the placid faced Android move the stone over Jarod's stiff posture.

At first Jarod noticed nothing, but as the moments passed, a warm sensation flooded through his body. A swirling mass of color enveloped him in its multi-faceted embrace as his strength gathered. Within the swirling core, his mind and thoughts crystallized, infusing him with a sense of well-being.

Razzune smiled and waved a hand at the servers awaiting his signal. Tension broken, voices once again blended in conversation as men and women dressed in white tunics began bringing platters of food to the table. Soft music and savory food created an atmosphere of congeniality as others joined them. Sugared wines from far galaxies flowed from exotic decanters decorated in brilliant colors. Baskets filled with fruit and nuts lined the table, their fragrance like sweet honey. Meat that Jarod had never tasted before delighted his taste buds. As he lifted slice after slice to his mouth, tender juices, seasoned with herbs, passed over his palate. "What is this?" he asked, pointing his fork at his plate.

"It is called venison," Razzune responded, "I'm so glad you enjoy it."

"I've never heard of venison," Jarod continued. "What planet does it come from?"

A faint smile touched Razzune's lips. "A planet the like of which you have never seen."

As he observed the many faces around him, Jarod realized they were a happy and animated people. Kraft and Myra were staring at each other like moonstruck kids. His thoughts wandered to Jessica. *I suppose it wouldn't hurt to be a little friendlier.*

When the meal ended, Myra indicated to Kraft that she must return to Jessica. She slipped out of her chair and hurried from the room to check on her charge. Jessica had awakened and was finishing off the last few bites of food left for her. Her hair was disheveled, but she looked rested and poised.

"Myra, I'm glad you're back. I was wondering if I might be able to shower and change clothes? By the way, the food was delicious." Jessica yawned and stretched. "I feel as though I'd slept the moon around."

"You do look refreshed," Myra said, a knowing smile touching her lips. "These are my living quarters. Please feel free to help yourself to anything. You will find the shower in the next room, I'll bring you something to wear." She eyed Jessica's tall slender figure. "I think I have just the thing."

To her amazement, Jessica found the shower poured forth real water. It was warm and wonderful. She lifted a dainty jar from the shelf and emptied a small amount of its contents into her palm. It smelled of the rare oil of EeGarion. Her skin glistened as she applied it to her body. Another drop she swept through her hair letting the fragrance wash over her face and neck. Humming a tune she hadn't heard in years, she wondered, *Where did that come from? I haven't thought about that since...since...*she paused, *since father taught it to me as a child.*

"I've placed a garment on the bed for you." Myra's voice interrupted her reverie.

"Thank you, I'll be right out."

"Please don't hurry. It sounds as though you are enjoying yourself."

Jessica sighed. "More than you know. I'd forgotten what it was like to feel a real water shower. Micro-showers can't compare with this." Reluctantly she turned off the water, lifted a long towel from its hook and draped it around her damp body as she stepped from the shower. Glancing in the mirror, she was shocked. Unbelieving, she swiped her hand over the moist surface several times and stared hard at her reflection. "Oh, my God!"

Myra rushed in from the next room. "Are you all right?" Seeing the stunned woman's expression, she couldn't help laughing. "I forgot to tell you."

Jessica looked closer in disbelief. "How..."

"You've a beautiful face, Jessica, and it didn't need to be marred with all you've been through. I simply brought back what was already yours. I should have told you sooner. I do apologize."

Jessica touched her scalp where the scar had been. "It's gone, really gone. But how...?"

"Yes, isn't it wonderful," Myra said, ignoring Jessica's

question. "But please hurry and dress, we must join the others. The Ancients are due at any moment."

When Jessica and Myra entered the dining hall Jarod stood and gripped the back of his chair. Jessica was dressed in a long sensuous gown that shimmered like jewels along her slim form and settled in folds around the gold sandals on her feet. Two golden cords crossed between her breasts and encircled her narrow waist. Her auburn hair was piled high in ringlets and entwined with gold bands. Jarod's breath caught in his throat and he swallowed. *She's so beautiful.*

Kraft watched Jarod's expression. His eyes never left Jessica as she was escorted to the chair at Razzune's right. *The guy doesn't know what hit him.* Kraft smiled, his own eyes turned to Myra. In the short time he had known her, he had come to realize how much she meant to him. Raising his glass to his lips in a silent salute to his friend, he thought, *I wish the same for you, buddy.*

"How lovely you look," Razzune addressed Jessica. "Don't you agree?" he asked, turning his attention to Jarod who was trying his best not to reveal the true feelings that were surging through his body. When it came to women's affections he was no amateur; most women found him fascinating, but this one hadn't even given him the time of day and...

A wiry smile tweaked the edges of Razzune's lips as he repeated the question interrupting Jarod's thoughts. "Don't you agree?"

"Ah...ah yes, very," Jarod responded, clearing his throat and feeling like a damn fool for being caught off guard. The only way to redeem himself was to change the subject. Hoping his hesitation had gone unnoticed, he asked Razzune why Quad was not with them.

Jessica looked up sharply. "Quad? Quad is here? Why

wasn't I told? Where is he?" She started to rise from her chair but Razzune laid a restraining hand on her arm.

"Yes, he was here and you shall be told everything, but first I think Jarod should bring us up to date and explain what has happened." He motioned to Jarod. "Please."

Relived to be on a different subject, Jarod told how he, Kraft and Quad had come searching for Jessica when she hadn't show up at command headquarters as planned.

Jessica, anxious to reveal the true nature of Vantra's treachery, held her peace and waited for Jarod to finish.

"Quad's shoulder was dislocated in the crash of the tube. After I reset it I left him and went in search of Kraft, who was thrown from the wreckage. I didn't know if he was dead, or alive wandering in the tunnels out of his mind from feeder poisoning. That's when Kell here," he motioned to the man in question, "came along, and we began our search for Chaser Calder. The rest, of course, you know." Turning back to Razzune, he asked, "Now what's happened to Quad?"

"You did an excellent job of resetting his shoulder," Razzune said. "The stone simply completed the healing. He has returned to Pragora to bring his family to Sanctuary. Two of our men escorted him to your cruiser outside the mines and will await their return seeing them safely back here..."

Jessica broke in. "Why would he want to bring Augueen and the boys here? Quad wouldn't have left in the first place knowing I was still missing!" Her voice was trembling. She stared hard at Razzune. "What kind of influence do you have over these people anyway?" There was too much she didn't understand and Razzune's lack of answers made her all the more determined to get to the truth.

Myra moved from her chair and lightly touched Jessica's shoulder. "Please, Jessica, trust us. We mean you or Jarod no harm. Kraft can vouch for that. If we were to lift a hand against either of you he would be the first to your defense."

Jessica glanced at Kraft sitting quietly with his hands folded in front of him. He smiled and winked.

"Yes, I suppose you're right," she said, relaxing. "You've been nothing but kind to me and I should be grateful. It's just that…" she hesitated, "I've become suspicious of people's motives."

Myra squeezed her shoulder sympathetically. "I understand. You've been through so much. Won't you please tell us what happened; how you came to be lost in the mines?"

Jessica thought for a moment then nodded affirmatively. "The night before I boarded the Glennden I was attacked by a man I had sent to prison five years ago. I believe he was somehow connected with Vantra's plot to kidnap me; however his desire for revenge must have been stronger than his orders and he tried unsuccessfully to kill me." Jessica unconsciously moved her fingers along the smooth ridge of her temple where Protandel had left his mark.

"I also believe the third officer aboard the Glennden was involved as well. He seemed to know an awful lot about why I was going to Zeer. He was also the one in charge of transporting me down to Pragora. Instead I found myself being held prisoner in the caves by a giant of a man called Naal."

Jarod flinched and clenched his fist. "Naal's a vicious killer; a mercenary who hires out to the highest bidder and will do anything for a price. We tracked him several times, but he always managed to give us the slip."

"He won't be giving anyone the slip," Jessica said, "I managed to overpower him in my cell, and in the struggle he impaled himself on his own blade." Her eyes hardened. "I only wish I'd been the one to plunge the knife." Her voice was bitter.

"I found out he tortured my father under Vantra's orders." Tears welled behind her eyes, but she fought for control holding them at bay. "Vantra came to my cell and bragged about the fact that my father's death was no accident."

"But why should Prince Vantra want to imprison you?" Myra asked.

"He kept talking about a portal he was determined to get his hands on, even if it meant killing me," Jessica answered.

Myra glanced at Razzune, her expression cautious.

Jessica continued. "I believe Vantra's aim is to find this so-called portal and destroy all of you. I don't know what connection you have in all this but if it has anything to do with destroying Vantra, I'm with you."

Razzune stood and paced, one hand cupping his beardless chin, the other resting behind his back. "I went to Prince Vantra representing our people, demanding he make public the documents taken from the Archives of Ancient History; documents that would make all men equal and independent of one ruler, free to choose their own government. Vantra was enraged and ordered all Eternians to be rounded up and imprisoned for insurrection, using the guise we were rebelling because we refuse to acknowledge his Age of Enlightenment. That was partially true, but we knew Vantra was afraid that if the New Earthians realized the truth within those documents, his rulership would be at risk. We were a threat to his power and he used the fact that we would not conform as a ruse against us."

Gripping the back of his chair, Razzune steadied himself. "But now his motives have become far more sinister. He is ruthless and I believe he has discovered our secret and will stop at nothing to make it his own."

"What secret?" Jessica said, bolting upright. "Does this have anything to do with my father's death? You'd better tell me, Razzune, I'm tired of all the half-truths you and Kell have been feeding us. Just what do you know?"

Razzune held out both hands in a gesture of appeal. He sighed, and dropped back into his chair. "Yes, of course," he said, smiling wanly at Jessica. "You are entitled to know the sacrifice your father made to keep the secret entrusted to him by the Ancients. Not only your father, but also Jarod's grandfather." He folded his hands and rested them on the table. "Your destinies are bound together." He shrugged. "But it is the Ancients, not I, who must reveal the answers you seek."

"Then where the hell are they?" Jarod snapped, his peaceful mood evaporating as fast as it had begun. "And stop discussing *my* destiny as though I'm not in the same room!" He kicked back his chair and stood to his feet startling Razzune and the others. Anger flared on his face as he bent over the table, pressing both palms to its slate surface, looking hard at Razzune. "I'll be the one to take care of my own future and I don't need the Ancients or anyone else deciding who I'll share it with!"

He is rather appealing, Jessica thought amusedly, surveying his rugged profile, *especially when he's mad.*

Sensing her eyes on him, Jarod glared at her, but Jessica quickly looked away in all innocence and fingered the wine glass by her plate.

Realizing his outburst had only made him look foolish, Jarod moved from the table as though to leave.

Kraft, who hadn't missed a thing, noted the expression on Jessica's face as she watched Jarod. Her lips were slightly parted and there was a flush to her checks. Grinning lopsidedly, he nudged Myra and whispered in her ear, "I think they just need a little encouragement."

Myra sighed. "We must see what we can do." She squeezed his hand beneath the table.

Chapter 21
The Ancients

Candles flickered casting shadowy movement over the domed ceiling. The soft stirring of air wafted through the room growing stronger as though someone had opened a door to the outside. A spiraling sphere of light appeared high in the dome growing in intensity and size as it descended coming to rest above the table. The room was hushed.

Like mannequins from some ancient storefront three bodiless beings took shape within the pulsating orb. Their eyes, imbedded in deep gray sockets, were covered with a silvery membrane accentuating the metallic shading of their hairless skulls. Lipless mouths gave the appearance of having been sliced into the skin with a sharp instrument. Gray membrane covered the small opening on either side of their large heads, indicative of what once might have been ears. The Ancients spoke.

"We are by nature telepathic, but for the benefit of all we will speak with human voices. Since we are one, we speak as one." They addressed Jarod first. "We are pleased to see you, Jarod, it has been a while." Their synchronized voices echoed slightly with a heavy accent.

Then they turned to Jessica who continued fingering her wineglass, tracing moist condensation along its bowl. "And you, Chaser Caldar, have served the Federation well." Jessica calmly waited, viewing the Ancients with suspicion. Reading her thoughts, the slightest suggestion of a smile parted their mouths. "We understand your suspicions. You are wondering why we want to help the Eternians, while at the same time advising Prince Vantra's Council of Six. Our motives, as you will see, have much to do with our past." The orb shifted slightly.

"Like yourselves, we were once human. Thousands of years before New Earth was colonized our race lived on the planet Trykona, located in the star belt, Cloist. It was a place of beauty, peace and plenty. With lush green valleys fed by flowing rivers, sustaining every kind of plant imaginable. Animals roamed freely through forested shelters. We were a free people, happy and content. Our knowledge was far beyond anything your world could imagine. We built machines that could harness wormholes enabling us to travel throughout the universe in seconds, jumping from one galaxy to another, visiting planet after planet. Hundreds of generations later we elders began to evolve into a higher form of intelligence. We no longer needed food to sustain us. Our bodies became cumbersome and awkward and we shed them for what you see before you now. Communication became telepathic and…"

"Get to the point." Kraft spoke up impatiently. "What's that got to do with why we're here?"

Myra nudged him. "Let them continue," she said softly.

"I dammed will if they'll just tell us!"

Myra smoothed the back of her hand across his cheek. "Patience, dear."

"She's right," Jarod said evenly, returning to his chair. "Let's hear what they have to say."

Kraft, clearly frustrated, murmured something unintelligible.

Jessica wished she could move around, her back was aching from sitting so long. She shifted in her chair causing the material of her gown to shimmer in the light. Jarod's attention was drawn to the golden cords crossing between the swell of her breasts. His gaze rose to the pulse in her throat, then slowly, sensuously, he lifted his eyes to hers.

Jessica brought up her chin in defiance and forced herself to meet his hungry stare. She felt herself being drawn into the whirlpool of his gray eyes. She tried to pull away but his gaze held her. The room was stifling. She wet her lips. It was as though every ounce of breath were being squeezed from her body. She fought to escape, but at the same time she had the overwhelming desire to experience that same hunger for herself. The feel of his touch, his arms about her.... *This is insane!* Her thoughts became a maze of contradictions carrying her into a maelstrom of confusion. Was she falling in love with Jarod Krinner? No! No! Impossible. He was not the kind of man she wanted. He was arrogant, self-centered and...

The Ancients' thought pattern sliced through Jessica's whirling mind releasing her from Jarod's unsettling spell. He turned away reluctantly, a faint smile creasing his lips. He was satisfied for the moment. The fire had been lit. Jessica, seeing the smile was seething inside. *Of all the...*

"You are impulsive, Commander Taybor," the Ancients continued, speaking as one, breaking into Jessica's mental tirade. "But you shall have your answer. And, Jessica, the words you were about to use do not suit you." She had forgotten the Ancients could read her mind. Oh, God! They had witnessed her intimate desire.

The orb shifted again, moving the encased features of the

Ancients into profile, their sphere gently floating above the table as their single voice continued to resonate.

"A marauding band of Saroaks were accidentally sucked through one of the wormholes into our galaxy and discovered Trykona. They enslaved many of our people and methodically killed off those who remained, leaving our planet desolate and shattered. We were not a warring people and therefore had no defensive weapons. Before all perished, three elders were selected to escape and take with them the secret we have guarded for generations. The ability to create a new world. Those chosen to leave Trykona were to receive the Prophecy and become guardians of a new generation that would arise, called Eternians."

"My God, they're talking about you and the others," Kraft said, turning to Myra.

"Yes," she said, her violet eyes beaming. "Isn't it wonderful? Not only we Eternians, but also all those who refuse to follow Prince Vantra. But let them continue." She turned to face Jessica and Jarod. "You must know the whole story."

"You've known all along," Kraft said, his voice accusing.

"Yes," Myra answered, touching him tenderly. "But it was not for me to reveal."

Slowly rotating, the Ancients once again singled out Jarod. "We were chosen to escape and brought with us the Prophecy as well as the secret to this new world. Our search brought us into your star system and to New Earth. There we discovered the people we were looking for, the Eternians. It was as the Prophecy was written.

"Your grandfather, Kardon Faus, was our first contact. He was a good man and ruled New Earth with peace and justice. In time we were accepted as his advisors. The Eternians were safe for the moment, or so we thought. But your grandfather

142

was assassinated and Bardas Vantra took his place. In the Prophecy it was revealed that a ruler would come into power, one who would try to destroy the Eternians. We continued to serve your Federation biding our time until we could safely transport all Eternians to the new world."

The Ancients addressed Jessica. "One man shared our secret; a scientist who refused to work for Vantra in his genetic engineering experiments."

"My father," Jessica interjected, straightening in her chair, her eyes intent. "He hated Vantra's cloning experiments." Her voice hardened. "Men without souls turned into BorCrons. Father swore he would never use his knowledge against any living being."

"And that is why we chose him to build Legend, and Kell, his counterpart."

"You mean to tell me my father created this...this..." she pointed at Kell, "Android?" She was incredulous. "He would have told me...Legend would have told me..."

Razzune, who had sat silently observing, stepped to her side. "Your father felt it was safer if you didn't know." He rested his hand on her shoulder. "Unlike Legend, Kell would be free to move between the two worlds. As a replicater he was able to change his appearance and go undetected by the BorCron sensors."

Jessica frowned up at Razzune. "Legend seemed to know nothing about the Eternians. He was as curious as I was when Kell appeared at the hovertrain." Her tone was defensive. "He wouldn't have kept the truth from me."

"He didn't," Razzune said, returning to his chair. "He was programmed to withhold certain information from you."

"Would someone please explain who this Legend is?" Jarod said. "And what he has to do with all this?"

Jessica had been so frustrated she had forgotten Jarod and

Kraft were unaware of Legend's existence. Too late she realized her mistake. There was nothing for it but to explain. "Legend is a computer of artificial intelligence, but more than that he's my friend, and the only family I have left. My father gave him human thought and emotions, even his own voice. If it hadn't been for Legend I don't know how I would have made it through the long months after my father's death." She hurt thinking about it even now. What Razzune had to say hurt her even further.

"Your father was betrayed by his lab assistant, Weston Steiner. Steiner found out about the portal, that it opened the way to a new planet, and went to Vantra. Vantra schemed to take control of the portal, but when Steiner failed to learn its whereabouts, Vantra had your father tortured, then disposed of him, along with Steiner."

Jessica moaned. "Oh, God, that's what Weston was trying to tell me in the hospital after the explosion." She rubbed her hands up and down her arms as though the room had suddenly turned cold. "Vantra thought I knew where the portal was and concocted this whole disappearing act so I would be brought to Pragora to look for him." Her lips tightened. "That means his Council knew all along, and if they knew..." her eyes darkened as she lifted them to the Ancients, "...they knew as well."

Razzune intervened, "Before you draw any conclusions, remember the Ancients were not with the Council at all times. Vantra chose to exclude them most of the time."

"It is natural you should suspect us of treachery," the Ancients said. "The only way we could thwart Vantra's plan was to continue as advisers to his Council of Six. Our first concern, of course, was for the people we had been sent to rescue. We were able to convince the Council we were dedicated to Vantra. At the same time we dispatched Kell with the Prophecy to the Eternians. Unfortunately, he and the others were caught up in the BorCron raid and brought here to the caves. For ten years now, every one, including Vantra, has been under the illusion they are still imprisoned in these mines. But many have been transported through the portal to Eterna."

"You mean people are already living on this...this new planet?" Kraft asked, surprised.

"Yes. Almost all," Razzune answered for the Ancients. "We at Sanctuary are the last, with the exception of your chief, Jessica," he said, nodding in her direction. "He and his family will be here soon, then we will join the others."

Jessica's brows knit together. "And if we refuse to go?"

"You will have nothing to return to. New Earth is doomed," he answered.

"This is insane!" Jarod stood and looked around at the many faces observing him intently. "Why a new world? You have powers, why not just rid New Earth of Vantra. Save us all this idiocy!"

"Because," the Ancients returned, "New Earth is about to be destroyed."

"What. Again?" Kraft mocked. "You'd think once would be enough."

Myra turned to him her eyes aflame with anger. "How dare you ridicule what you don't understand. They speak the truth, New Earth *is* doomed!" She looked hard at Kraft. "I thought you of all people would listen, but instead I find I've fallen in love with a fool!" Her chair scraped the floor as she jumped to her feet and fled the room in tears.

"Now look what you've done," Jessica said, glaring accusingly at Kraft.

He looked bewildered. "I only meant..."

"To say," Jarod interrupted, "what the rest of us are thinking. What the hell are you talking about?"

Suddenly Kraft's face lit up. "Did you hear what she said? She loves me." He sprang to his feet and dashed after Myra.

Jarod stared after his friend in frustration then turned back to the Ancients. "All right, let's hear it."

"The asteroid shower that devastated Earth in 2025 will be nothing compared to the asteroid which will hit in fifty-two hours. Its surface is ten times that of New Earth. The protective domes, held in place by giant computers, will disintegrate leaving the planet exposed to the poisonous atmosphere. New Earth will be rocked off its axis. Gasses within its core will implode, and New Earth will nova. This time there will be no survivors."

Jessica jumped to her feet. "My God if that's true we have to warn them!"

"Your chief, Quad, is doing just that," Razzune said. "He has gone to get his family and send messages to the Federation and the Council of Six."

"Why the hell didn't you tell us this to begin with!" Her voice was hard and accusing.

Kell stepped forward. "Because Quad knew there wasn't time to waste. He asked me to find you and Jarod and said to do what ever it took to keep you both here. He knew you would try to follow, but for anyone to go after him now would be fruitless. He has taken the cruiser and there's no other way to cross the wasteland."

"If anything happens to him or his family," Jessica flared, "I'll take that Android hide of yours apart, piece by piece!"

"And if she doesn't, I will!" Jarod interjected.

"Please, please," Razzune pleaded. "Enough of this quarreling. Quad has assured us he will do everything within his power to warn New Earth and bring his family here. We must work together. We cannot prevent the inevitable, but we can begin a new future on Eterna. A new generation, free from the tyranny of such men as Bardas Vantra." He folded his hands and looked inquiringly at the Ancients. "Should you not now tell Jarod?"

"This is insane. I've heard enough," Jessica fumed. "I'm going to my room." Jarod watched her, thinking to himself as she moved down the hallway; *She's up to something.* He turned back to the Razzune. "Tell me what?"

The Ancients spoke. "At the age of seventeen, three years after your grandfather, Kardon Faus, was assassinated, you were taken to Eterna and trained by Kell. But those memories were erased from your mind until we determined you would make a worthy leader. Both your father and grandfather served the Federation with honor. We watched you over the years follow that same tradition. You have proven yourself well, Jarod. Now it is time to restore those memories."

Before Jarod could protest, gray eyes fixed him with their gaze, burrowing deep, drawing him like a magnet. Memories buried deep within his subconscious spewed to the surface like magma from a volcano. *Eterna. He was young, in his teens...Kell was with him...His mentor, trainer...*

Realization twisted his rugged features into stunned awareness as he was held transfixed. Eterna, a planet more beautiful than Early Earth had been before great cities of concrete and steel had destroyed her forests, and massive highway systems split her apart from continent to continent.

"Even so," Jarod said, his eyes hardening, their gray pigment darkening to steel, "what gives you the right to dictate my life!"

***

The spaceship Titan sped towards New Earth. Aboard her massive structure Prince Vantra paced her bridge, his mood as black as her hull.

No bodies had been found in the wreckage of the gravity tube. His BorCrons were still undertaking the massive task of searching the caves for Jessica and the others, but it would take time, time he didn't have. He couldn't keep up the charade if he was to maintain control of New Earth; he must return. A plausible explanation for his absence would be issued by his Council to appease the people, but in the meantime he would await word from the mines. "Damn the woman," he said between clenched teeth.

"Inform the Council of my arrival," he instructed the captain. His vanity had been the motivation for their cloning, but according to his high opinion of himself, they fell far short. *I'll replace them soon*, he thought. The idea appealed to him and he smiled maliciously.

The captain interrupted his thoughts. "Your Highness, the Council awaits your orders."

"Put them on screen."

The Council of Six bowed in unison. "Your Highness." One man stepped forward, his hands hidden within the folds of his robe, his eyes downcast in homage as he addressed his leader. "We look forward to—"

"Yes, yes," Vantra interrupted, waving his hand impatiently. "Have Chaser Caldar's living quarters searched. Tear the place apart if you have to."

"What is it you wish found?" the man asked.

"Anything having to do with the portal. Ryden Caldar may have left something with her."

"Then your mission was not a success?" Too late the man realized his mistake. Fear generated through his body as he raised his eyes to Vantra. He tried to compensate. "That is, I mean..."

Vantra snarled obscenities at him. "Send my BorCrons to Caldar's as I instructed. I'll deal with you later!"

***

Terrell Mackly, first officer of the BorCron Directive, glanced around at the carnage of Jessica's lodgings. Every piece of furniture had been ripped apart and piled in heaps around the various rooms. The hologram that had once displayed scenic pictures of Early Earth had been destroyed. Even the artificial pond had been drained and crushed. The only places left untouched were the walls and floor. They were next.

"Bring in the blaster," Mackly ordered.

Legend waited. As the walls shattered and black shielded forms spilled into the secret lab his console sprang to life.

"Sir," one of his men shouted, "it's dispatching a message!"

"Well stop it!" Mackly shouted back.

Gloved hands frantically punched commands into Legend's keyboard. "It's not responding!"

"Then use your laser, dammit, destroy the thing!"

The blast tore through Legend's console ripping apart his instrument panel. A single word flashed across his screen before exploding into a thousand pieces. JESSICA.

"Search every inch of this room," Mackly ordered, kicking at the shattered remains.

***

The Ancients had departed the dining hall leaving Jarod pacing angrily, his strides taking him from one end of the table to the other.

Kell and Razzune were standing off to the side talking in low tones. Suddenly Kell stiffened. His head went up as though listening intently.

"What is it?" Razzune asked.

Kell flashed a quick glance at Jarod. His voice was low. "It's Legend."

"What about Legend?"

"He's been destroyed."

Razzune's eyes widened. He thought of Jessica. "Legend was the only family she had. I can't imagine what this will do to her." His voice was sympathetically sad. "She's suffered so much trauma already."

"Leave it to me," Kell responded.

"The way things are between you two I don't believe that's a good idea," Razzune said. "I had best be the one to tell her."

"Very well," Kell replied. "Fortunately Legend was able to download everything before the BorCrons destroyed his mainframe."

"Then you have the instructions?" Razzune asked, breathing easier.

"Yes," Kell replied, "I've converted them to a chip." Turning slightly, he pushed aside his shirt and opened a small portion of his chest. Electrodes flashed as he freed the chip and handed it to Razzune.

"I'd appreciate it if someone would show me to Kraft's room," Jarod said, ceasing the agitated pacing. His anger was somewhat subdued, but threatened to boil to the surface again if he didn't get away to think.

"Of course," Razzune responded, turning away from Kell and approaching Jarod. "I apologize for keeping you. It has been a trying day for all of us. Dane," he beckoned to one of the men, "please escort Chaser Krinner to Commander Kraft's room."

***

Pausing to knock gently at Myra's door, Jessica listened for approaching footsteps to tell her Myra was present. Receiving no answer, she pushed the door open and stepped into the softly illuminated interior. She called out Myra's name, but was greeted with silence. *Must be with Kraft,* she thought. Her uniform, cleaned and mended, lay neatly folded on the bed. Removing the evening gown, she carefully hung it in the closet then slipped into her uniform. It felt reassuring, more like herself. She brushed out the tight crown of curls and swept back her auburn hair, securing it with a ribbon from one of the drawers. *I shouldn't be missed until I'm well out of the caves. I've got to make it back to New Earth.* Talking about Legend had made her realize more than ever her need to save him. Even as she had been speaking about him to the others, her mind was forming a plan to escape Sanctuary and return to New Earth to rescue her friend. She would remove his programming disk and rebuild him when it was safe.

Myra's room opened onto a small patio. Jessica slipped out into the twilight created by the dimmed lights atop the crystal building and moved stealthily along the pathway that ran adjacent to the reflecting pool. The fragrance of flowers drifted on the warm air and gentle ripples murmured from the pool. The crunch of gravel warned her someone else was on the path ahead of her and moving in her direction. Jerking her head from side to side, she hurriedly searched for a place to hide, but the hedge of flowers was too low making concealment impossible. All she could do was wait.

"I gather from the way you're dressed, you're not just out for a stroll?"

Damn, of all people it would be him.

She tried to move around Jarod, but he blocked her. "Get out of my way!"

He gripped her arm as she tried to pass and lowered his head so that his mouth was close to her ear, his voice smooth. "Do you really think you can make it out of these caves alone?"

"Let go of me! What business is it of yours what I do!" She struggled to break his hold, but he swung her around to face him, his hands squeezing her upper arms tightly.

"You little fool. I'm making it my business!"

To her complete surprise, Jarod pulled her into an embrace and lowered his mouth to hers. At first his kiss was harsh, as though he wanted to punish her. She struggled to push him away but he pressed her closer. Her mind told her to fight, but her body began sending signals of surrender. A myriad of sensual sensations pulsated through her as Jarod's lips moved over hers drawing her deeper into the fire of his passion. He raised his head slightly, his breath warm against her cheek. "I've wanted to do this for a long time," he whispered, slowly tracing the curve of her neck with his mouth, lingering at the pulse in her throat; the place he had wanted to explore as he sat watching her across the table earlier. Jessica sighed and raised her arms to encircle his neck, her fingers locking themselves in his hair. Her head was thrown back, her face flushed, her breath caught in her throat.

"Ahumm...am I interrupting anything?" Kraft stood with arms crossed, grinning from ear to ear.

Jarod raised his head and glared at Kraft over Jessica's shoulder.

She freed herself from his embrace and moved to a bench close to the reflecting pool. She was embarrassed, but more than that, confused. She had abandoned herself to Jarod's lovemaking, her passion as strong as his.

"What is it that's so important it couldn't wait?" Jarod snarled at Kraft, thinking about how he would like very much to toss his friend into the reflecting pool.

"I wanted to be the first to tell you, Myra has agreed to marry me and we want you to perform the ceremony."

"Congratulations," Jarod said sarcastically, "but I'm a Chaser not a judge."

"You're a Chaser on this planet, but when you go to Eterna you'll be a leader and able to marry us. So what'da you say, pal?"

"What is he talking about?" Jessica asked, rising from the bench, her thoughts pushed to the background with this new revelation.

Kraft turned to face Jessica. "Word has it that the Ancients have selected Jarod to be the Eternians new leader." He turned back to Jarod. "So that means you can perform the ceremony."

"What makes you so sure I have any intention of going to Eterna?" Jarod was irritated that Kraft had brought up the subject in front of Jessica. "Everyone seems to think they know what my plans are!" Jarod brushed his fingers through his hair. "I'd appreciate it if you and the others would mind your own damn business!"

"That's not the first time you've told me to mind my own business," Kraft laughed, "but face it, it's never gonna happen."

"If you two will excuse me, I'll return to my room." Jessica looked directly at Jarod. "It's been amusing." He frowned, wondering what was going through that stubborn head of hers; somehow he didn't think it was good. In fact, if he had been privy to her thoughts, he would have known his lovemaking had not deterred her in the slightest from planning to rescue Legend.

Myra was seated on the couch when Jessica stormed into the room. She was about to tell Jessica of Kraft's marriage proposal when she stopped short, her voice full of concern. "What's wrong? Are you all right? You look..."

"Angry?" Jessica finished for her. "That arrogant man thinks he can charm me like all the other women in his life." Of course she had no idea how many women he might have had, but her tirade continued, "Like I'm some soft-headed female who can't resist his advances!"

Myra couldn't help smiling. "Come sit with me," she said, patting the place next to her. Jessica hesitated; she wanted to be alone to form a plan to leave Sanctuary. Alerted now, Jarod might attempt to prevent her, but she had to try.

However, Myra was insistent, so reluctantly Jessica sat down. Myra took her hands. "Jarod is not the man you make him out to be, Jessica. Kraft has told me so much about his friend I feel I know him. He's no angel, nor is Kraft, for that matter, but I've seen the way Jarod looks at you, and…"

Jessica pulled away and stood to her feet. She didn't want to hear it. Looking down at Myra, she frowned. "Of course you'd see him through his friend's eyes," she said, "you're in love with Kraft."

Myra's voice was soft. "I'm not blind, Jessica, I've watched the two of you, and whether you want to admit it or not, you *are* in love with Jarod."

Jessica turned her back to Myra, her shoulders slightly slumped, as though Myra's words bore a heavy weight. Reaching forth her hand to touch one of the green plants, she smoothed a leaf between her thumb and fingers, then turning she dropped back onto the couch with a sigh. "I'm confused, Myra. There is an attraction, but at the same time he infuriates me. When he kissed me just now, I felt as though there was no one I'd rather be with."

Myra's eyes twinkled as she reached to pat Jessica's hand. "I know, that's exactly how I felt the first time Kraft kissed me. You're confused because you've never experienced real passion before." Myra leaned closer. "If it's anything like what I feel for Kraft, you needn't worry."

Jessica laughed, her frustration eased. Myra had become a friend she felt she could trust. "Myra, I've got to leave Sanctuary to save my friend, Legend." Her expression became intense. "Will you help me?"

Chapter 22
Warning

Before Jessica's rescue, two of the Eternians had guided
Quad through the tunnels and back to the gravity tube
entrance. One of the men now spoke. "You have five hours.
We will wait here for your return."

Quad nodded and traversed the open space to where Kraft
had parked the hyper-cruiser alongside one of the empty
barracks. The wind was sharp and he ducked his head to
avoid gritty sand invading his eyes. Red moon was at its
zenith and the cold was bitter. Even his thermo suit couldn't
completely block out the chill. He climbed into the cockpit
and started the boosters. Lifting off he circled the cave once
then headed out over the Pragorian wasteland.

The flight took less than an hour, allowing him time to
meditate on what had transpired over the past twenty hours:
his encounter with Kell in the tunnel, the healing stone, and
most of all, Eterna. It had taken a great deal of persuasion on
the Ancients part to convince him of the ultimate destruction
of New Earth, but now he was headed back to the command
post at Pragora to warn the Federation, and Vantra's Council

of Six of the impending disaster. He had less than five hours to get the message to them, and convince Augueen that she and their sons must return with him to Sanctuary. He hoped Kell was successful in locating Jarod and Jessica.

Gliding the cruiser onto the tarmac, Quad brought it to a stop just short of the hanger. He jumped from the cockpit and sprinted across the tarmac to the communications building. Augueen and his sons were housed in an adjacent building, but he would have to forgo seeing them until the others were warned.

"Floor requested?" the computer asked as Quad stepped into the elevator.

"Ten," Quad replied, impatiently shifting his large frame as he watched the numbers fly by.

"Tenth floor." The computer's tone was clipped and official. "You are entering a restricted area. Prepare to be scanned."

Quad exited the elevator and approached a scan pad to the left of the door marked, COMMUNICATIONS—AUTHO-RIZED PERSONNEL ONLY. He pressed his palm against the pad listening for the click as the door unlocked. He stepped through into an outer office where an overfed cadet sat at a cluttered desk stained with coffee rings. Even the partially open window failed to eliminate the stale smell of cigarettes and bad breath. Quad shot a disdainful look at the man and marched past him towards the communications room.

The man jumped to his feet and circled around the desk to intercept Quad. "Sir, you can't go in there!" Quad brushed him aside.

"What...the...hell!" Ryan, the Communications Officer, whirled around as Quad burst through the door, the frustrated cadet in full pursuit. "Walker, what's this man doing in here? Call security!"

Quad strode into the room and proceeded to punch in codes on one of the computers, ignoring Ryan's attempt to stop him. Walker stood dumfounded, but sprang to life when Ryan bellowed at him, "WALKER!"

"This should satisfy you as to my identity," Quad said, stepping back from the computer. "My credentials."

Ryan glared suspiciously at Quad then stepped forward to examine the screen. "WALKER, LEAVE OFF THAT ORDER!" Walker, who had just notified security, looked annoyed and repeated the order into the intercom. He plunked down behind his desk and lit up a cigarette. Puffs of smoke curled around his disgruntled face.

"What can I do for you, sir? If you had let me know instead of bursting in like that…"

"I don't have time to explain everything, Officer…" Quad squinted at Ryan's nametag…"Officer Ryan. I've got to get messages to the Federation and Vantra's Council. An asteroid ten times bigger than New Earth will hit in less than fifty-two hours, they've got to be evacuated."

"Sir, Mars base Tros has been tracking the asteroid for some time now and they say it will miss Earth by at least a thousand miles."

"Well they're wrong! *When*, not *if* it hits, there won't be any survivors unless the Federation sends rescue ships."

Ryan stiffened. "I don't know where you got your information, sir, but I'd be inclined to believe Tros's satellites."

"Then you're a fool!" Quad turned his back to Ryan and sat at a Vid-Com. He began sending simultaneous messages to all the colonies on New Earth and to the Federation. Lastly he brought up Vantra's Council of Six.

"What do you think you're doing, Quad?" One of the Six stood scowling into the screen. "You were sent to Pragora to help Jarod Krinner locate Chaser Caldar, not create panic with this misinformation concerning the asteroid." The Vantra clone turned and acknowledged the other five. "We are well aware of its existence and there is no danger to New Earth." The others nodded in agreement. "You are to return immediately and present yourself before this Council."

"Sorry, but I can't do that. I don't think you'll be seeing Krinner or Caldar either. I've given you fair warning. What you choose to do with it is up to you, but I would advise you to take a closer look at that satellite. Off." Quad sat for a moment before the blank screen then rose and headed for the door. *God help them*, he thought.

***

Augueen sat mending one of Retsel's shirts when Quad entered their quarters. "Quad." She quickly put aside the shirt and rushed to him. "You're safe. I was so worried when I didn't hear from you." She looked up into his face and saw the concern. "What's wrong? Is Jessica all right?" Fear threaded its way into her amber eyes.

He nudged his cheek against hers, as was the Borkian way of showing affection. "She's not been found yet. Chaser Krinner and Kell are searching the caves. It's just a matter of time."

Augueen looked puzzled. "Kell? Who is Kell?"

Quad pulled her to the couch and sat with her hands nestled in his. Nudging her cheek once again he said, "I have something to tell you."

He began with the events that led up to his encounter with Kell, then about Sanctuary and the Ancients. Augueen sat quietly listening until he came to the Ancients prediction of the destruction of New Earth.

"Oh, Quad, all those people." She broke free and sprang to her feet staring down at him in horror. "Our friends, we must warn them!" It never entered her mind to doubt him, she knew him too well.

"I've done that, Augueen," Quad said, joining her. "I've contacted everyone I can think of including the Federation, as well as Vantra's Council."

"Then they will evacuate New Earth?" she asked hopefully.

"No. The idiots won't listen. They assure me their satellites are closely tracking the asteroid and it will miss New Earth by at least a thousand miles." His eyes turned steely. "New Earth will be destroyed, Augueen, and there's nothing we can do about it."

"Maybe the Ancients are mistaken. Maybe the asteroid...will...veer...off..." Her voice trailed away. Looking into Quad's eyes she knew he was right, but she didn't want to believe it. Tears spilled over her cheeks.

Quad held his wife and waited for her tears to subside. "We have less than four hours to return to Sanctuary." He brushed her wet cheeks with his fingers and held her face between his hands. "We'll start a new life on Eterna with the others."

Augueen stiffened. Pulling away from his embrace, she shook her head. "Eterna? But why there? Why not go home to Borkia? We're not the same race. We don't know them." She looked pleadingly at him, her voice strained and halting.

"Did we know the Earth people before we went there?" he said flatly.

Augueen turned away and moved gracefully towards the window despite her heavy heart. Her gown made a rustling sound as she crossed the room. Standing with hands clasped in front of her she gazed down at the tarmac two stories below. Several people were scrambling across the field, insulated hoods pulled tight over their heads against the cold. A young cadet stood at stiff attention being reprimanded by a superior officer. The words were inaudible from where she stood looking down, but from the stormy look on the officer's face she could not help but feel sorry for the cadet. Reaching a decision, she sighed, unclasped her hands, and retraced her steps back to Quad, who stood patiently waiting. She placed her hands on his shoulders and looked into his eyes. "You are my life, Quad. I cannot think of being anywhere else without you. We will go to Eterna."

Their two young sons, Condee and Retsel, who had been sleeping, were complaining at being awakened and forced to dress. "It's not time to get up," whined Retsel. Besides, Poom is still asleep." The small fury creature, curled into a tight ball on Retsel's bed, made twittering sounds in his sleep as though in full agreement.

Condee rubbed his eyes and asked, "Why do we have to get dressed? Are we going somewhere?"

The boys, just then realizing their father was in the room, jumped up and down with excitement, their Borkian clicks and hums growing louder and louder as their efforts to compete with each other broke into an argument.

"Enough," Quad said sternly. "It's time to leave. Take only what you can carry."

"But I can only carry Poom," Retsel cried.

"Here," Augueen said, "hand him to me."

When Retsel picked up Poom, the mocker squawked with indignation.

"Shush, you little rascal," Augueen said, folding him into her arm.

Chapter 23
Return

Condee and Retsel were thrilled to be flying in a Federation hyper-cruiser; it was difficult to contain their exuberance. Poom lay snug in Augueen's lap oblivious to all the excitement. Augueen was silent, keeping her thoughts to herself. Occasionally Quad would glance at his wife and wonder what was going through her mind.

Arriving at their destination, Quad made a slow descent to the barracks below. Alighting from the cruiser with the boys in tow, Augueen looked around anxiously surveying the desolate land that surrounded the barracks. She hugged herself. "It's so cold."

Quad reached into the interior of the cruiser and brought out thermo suits. "Here put these on." The lightweight material was easily adjusted so the boys had no problem fitting into theirs. Poom's ample fur was insulation enough against the severe cold, but Retsel tucked him into his jacket anyway.

Black Moon was ascending over the horizon, its inky shadow, like a vaporous cloud, plunging Zeer into intense darkness. Only the crackling sizzle of electric flashes gave off light as it split the air.

The family moved swiftly to the entrance of the tunnel where the two Eternians were waiting as planned. "We must hurry; there is activity in the caves." Quad assured them that his sensitive ears would be able to detect sounds long before they did. Quiet and subdued, Condee and Retsel huddled close to their mother's side. From time to time she reassured them with a gentle touch.

The small group traveled several hundred yards before emerging at the site where the gravity tube had crashed.

"I'm going to see if I can locate my laser," Quad said, dashing to the wreckage. The Eternians looked around warily, but before they could object he had climbed up the side of the tube and dropped out of sight.

"We must take cover," one of the men said. He led Augueen and the boys behind a large steel plate that had broken free from the wreckage. The other man stood watch.

Poom, objecting to being confined, wriggled from Retsel's jacket and scurried around the steel plate out into the open. He sat contentedly grooming himself.

A low droning strummed along the adjoining tunnel, growing louder as it neared their location. "BorCron tracers," the Eternians whispered in unison. The larger of the two crept over to Augueen. "Keep perfectly still, they won't fire their stun-lasers unless their sensors detect movement."

Two tracers whipped into the tunnel. Retsel pulled frantically on his mother's arm. "Mother, Poom!" Before she could stop him, Retsel darted from behind the steel plate to rescue his pet. The tracers fired, their stun blasts hitting the ground next to Retsel who was struggling to hold on to Poom.

Clots of dirt sprayed in every direction, some hitting Retsel in the face. Augueen screamed.

Condee was yelling and waving his arms, "Save him, Momma, save him!" The tracers snapped around ready to fire in Condee's direction. Quad jumped from the wreckage, laser in hand, firing again and again. The tracers' metal bodies splintered into pieces as each blast hit its mark.

Retsel, a look of horror on his young face, stood frozen to the spot clutching his terrified pet tightly to his chest. Quad rushed to his son and picked up the frightened boy. Tears were streaking down Retsel's dirt stained face. "I saved him, didn't I?" he said between sobs, holding Poom out for his father's inspection.

Quad smiled. "You sure did, son," he said, ruffling Retsel's hair, "you sure did."

Augueen ran to them and wrapped her arms around them both. She was shaking all over. "Oh, God, if you hadn't found your laser, I don't know what would have happened." She pulled Condee into their embrace. Poom squawked irritably.

"We must reach Sanctuary," the Eternian said. "The tracers will have disclosed our location to the BorCrons."

"Lead the way," Quad said, holding on to Retsel and motioning for his family to follow.

It took over an hour to reach their destination. The younger of the two Eternians stepped forward and pressed his hand into the indentation encircled by alien letters. The wall rippled and a gust of warm air swept over them as the way opened. Quad raised his hand, his body tense. Motioning to the Eternians, he shouted, "Quick, get them inside, it's the BorCrons!"

Shoving their son quickly into Augueen's arms, he yelled at her and the Eternians. "Go!" He stood waiting, legs splayed, laser in hand, his lidless eyes fiercely directed down the tunnel.

Chapter 24
BorCron Intrusion

About a dozen black shielded BorCrons spilled into the corridor. Quad fired several times hitting three of them squarely in the chest. A blaster hit the wall behind him, its concussion propelling Quad through the air. He landed hard on his back, but staggered up returning several more rounds before sprinting through Sanctuary's opening toward the crystal building. Lasers stung at his heels as he zigzagged across the walkway bridging the reflecting pool.

Kell stepped through the doorway, arms extended, blazing light flashing through his fingers. Several BorCrons dropped at once. A helmet flew from one of them, exposing the hideously deformed face.

"My family?" Quad hollered over the bedlam.

"They're safe," Kell shouted. "Go! I'll hold them off."

"Don't be a fool, there's too many!"

Jarod and Kraft came running from around the side of the building where they had been talking. Seeing the situation, they crouched down beside Quad.

"The BorCrons have broken through," he yelled at them,

firing on the advancing black shields. "There's nothing you can do here; get everyone to safety."

Jarod stubbornly held his ground but Quad glared at him and waved his arm. "Get the hell out of here and help the others!" Turning his back on them, he rushed to Kell's side. Lasers split the air as Quad and Kell continued firing.

"He's right," Kraft yelled at Jarod, pulling on his arm. "We're helpless without weapons."

They sprinted into the crystal building just as a terrain disintegrator tore through ahead of them toppling two of the columns in their path. Shards of crystal flew through the air narrowly missing them as they ducked their heads and dove behind an overturned piece of furniture.

"We can't stay here," Jarod said, "we're sitting ducks." He jumped to his feet and raced across the floor with Kraft hot on his heels. A barrage of firing followed them as they broke into the dining hall where Razzune was trying desperately to calm everyone.

Augueen and her sons were huddled together in a corner. She tried to keep her mind off what was happening outside, but fear was tearing at her heart. Swallowing to hold the tears at bay, she hugged Retsel and Condee closer reassuring them. "Don't be afraid, your father will be here soon; everything will be all right." She hoped it were true.

Kraft signaled for several of the men to help him drag the huge slate table across the floor. They heaved it onto its side and braced it against the door. "They've got terrain disintegrators," he said, running his arm over his sweating forehead. "I'm afraid this table isn't going to withstand that kind of power for long."

"Is this everyone?" Jarod asked, looking around at the frightened group. "Where are Jessica and Myra?"

Razzune looked worried. "I don't know. Jessica was

headed back to Myra's room the last time I saw her. I thought Myra was with Kraft."

Jarod shot a look in Kraft's direction. He was busy giving orders, directing the men to pile furniture on top of the table. He frowned. "I'll see if I can find them. You'd better get everyone to a safer spot."

"There's only one place left to go," Razzune said, "through the portal."

"Does Myra know where it is?" Jarod asked.

"Yes."

"Then get everyone there. We'll join you as soon as I find her and Jessica."

***

The two women in question ran from Myra's room into the hallway, colliding with a fleeing Eternian running in the opposite direction. Jessica grabbed the woman by the arm. "What's happening?"

"The BorCrons, they've broken through!"

Suddenly an explosion shook the building; lights flickered off, then on again. Jessica looked up and down the hallway. "Are there any weapons here?" she yelled at the terrified woman.

"No! Kell is the only one who can protect us."

Jessica remembered the Android's destruction of the feeder rats. "Damn! Then we've got to locate the others. Come on."

Leading the way, Jessica cautioned Myra and the other woman to stay close to the wall. Picking up a metal bar that had broken loose from one of the doors, Jessica moved guardedly down the corridor. Detecting movement coming along one of the adjoining hallways, she pressed a finger to her lips signaling the women to stay back while she went to investigate. Arm raised, bar ready to strike, she sprang into the corridor. Jarod jerked sideways as the bar came down just missing his head. He grabbed Jessica and propelled her backwards, both toppling to the floor with a thud, her body pinned beneath his. Jessica gasped as the wind was knocked out of her.

Faces only inches apart, Jarod found himself staring down into Jessica's blazing green eyes. "What...the...," he said.

"Get off me!" she yelled, pushing at him, her head jerking from side to side, struggling to free herself.

Jarod didn't move. "What, so you can bash my head in?"

"I thought you were a BorCron," she fired at him. "Now get off me!"

"Not before you toss that," he said, indicating the bar, figuring she might still use it on him.

"All right," Jessica flared, releasing the object. "Now if you don't mind!"

Releasing his grip, he pushed the bar away with the toe of his boot and slowly lifted his body from hers, savoring the moment, his eyes alight with amusement. Jessica brushed aside the hand he extended and angrily rose to her feet.

"Sorry," he said, sheepishly, brushing a hand through his hair. "Are you all right?"

"I'm fine," she answered sharply, straightening her uniform and whipping aside several strands of hair that had fallen across her cheek.

"I apologize," he said sincerely, hoping to make amends. "I was on my way to find you and Myra."

Myra, hearing his voice, came running up. The other woman followed. "Jarod, I'm so glad to see you...." She paused seeing Jessica's disheveled condition. "What happened?" she asked concerned.

Jessica glanced hard at Jarod. "I don't have time to explain right now."

"I've got to get you out of here," Jarod said. "Kell and Quad are holding off the BorCrons but it's only a matter of time before the place is overrun."

Jessica's head jerked up. "Then Quad made it back. What about his family?"

"They're with Razzune and the others," Jarod replied, noting her concern. "He's taking everyone to the portal room. I told him we'd join them there." He turned back to Myra. "Razzune said you knew the way."

Myra laid her hand on Jarod's arm. "Is Kraft..." Her voice faded, afraid to hear what Jarod might say.

"Fine..." he assured her, patting the small hand. "He loves you too much to get himself killed. We'd better get moving."

The smell of burning wood hung acrid in the air.

***

The thick steel door to the portal room slid open with a *whoosh*. Kraft sprinted across the floor and gathered Myra into his arms. Turning to Jarod, he smiled and said, "Thanks, pal, I knew you'd find her." He lifted Myra's hand to his lips and kissed it.

Prisms of color reflected off the stark walls. Their source, ten star shaped crystals embedded in the surface of a stone pedestal standing alone in the middle of the room. Jessica stepped close to examine it. Etched within the stone were indentations of two hand imprints and at the tip of each finger were the crystals. In the center of the pedestal rested a brilliantly lit globe surrounded with alien letters.

Myra freed herself from Kraft's embrace and came to stand by Jessica, whose eyes were concentrated on the flashing electrodes captured within the sphere.

"When Kell and Razzune place their hands in the indentations," Myra said, gently moving her hand over the pulsating light, "the portal will open. I pray they are safe and it's not too late."

The Eternians milled about, their voices subdued. Remembering Augueen, Jessica quickly scanned the room until she spotted her seated with her arms around Condee and Retsel. As she approached them, Augueen looked up, relief evident on her lovely face. "You're safe," she said, rising to hug Jessica. "I couldn't believe it when Quad told me you were missing. I was so worried." She stood back and looked at Jessica, her eyes full of concern. "Are you all right?"

"I'm fine," Jessica answered. *Why does everyone keep asking me that?* She bent down and spoke to the two frightened boys. "Don't worry, everything will be okay."

"Do you really think so?" Augueen asked, her voice strained.

Before Jessica could answer, Jarod's angry outburst drew their attention. "Why the hell did you let him go!"

Kraft's voice was raised in return. "I didn't *let* Razzune go; he was gone before I realized it!" Kraft nodded towards the Eternians. "It seems three of the women are unaccounted for."

"All right," Jarod said, calming down, placing a hand on Kraft's shoulder. "Stay here and take care of things, I'm going to see if I can find him." Moving towards the door, he muttered, "Dammit, why can't people stay put!"

Jessica hurried to his side. "I'm coming with you, and don't tell me no. I've got as much at stake in getting these people to safety as you do."

Knowing that standing here arguing with her while Razzune was wandering somewhere in the building would get him nowhere, he said flatly, "If we meet with any BorCrons don't expect me to rescue you."

"Wouldn't have it any other way," she threw back at him.

***

Intermittent firing sounded behind them as they moved from room to room. The crystal building was beginning to collapse. Blasters whizzed overhead tearing through the framework of Sanctuary. Close by BorCrons were searching through the rubble, their guttural voices raised above the destruction they were waging.

"We'd better separate." Jarod motioned for Jessica to go one way and he headed another.

He moved stealthily along the hallway keeping low to be less of a target. A BorCron passed within feet of him as he squatted behind a door dangling on its hinges. The temptation to down the man was strong, but he didn't want to take the chance of alarming any others that might be close by. Finding Razzune had to be his first priority. He wondered how Jessica was doing. *I should have kept her with me*, he thought, chiding himself for being such a hardhead. *I always manage to get on her wrong side.*

He was about to move out when he heard a low moan. Doubling back to where the sound came from, he found Razzune lying crumpled in a pool of blood, a laser wound to his chest. Jarod felt for a pulse. It was weak and Razzune's breathing was shallow. A blood trail along the floor told the story. Wounded, Razzune must have dragged himself this far before passing out. Jarod started to lift him, but Razzune opened his eyes and raised a feeble hand. "No...go...." Placing a shaking hand inside his robe he drew out a small chip. "Kell..." he said, his words labored, "knows..." Jarod leaned closer to catch what the wounded man was trying to say, but Razzune sighed and his body went limp.

Gently removing the chip from Razzune's hand, he slipped it into his pocket. "I'm not about to leave you here, old man," he said, gathering Razzune up into his arms.

As he stood to his feet a laser blast burrowed into the wall behind him, the heat searing away a portion of the wall. A BorCron stood in the doorway, his laser aimed at Jarod's head. With Razzune in his arms he was helpless. Movement behind the BorCron, and a flash of red hair signaled Jessica's presence. Her leg shot out catching the BorCron full in the back. The laser spun from his hand and he toppled to the floor. Jessica straddled his back, yanked off his helmet and with both hands, whipped the BorCron's head around, snapping his neck.

Jarod stared at her a look of admiration on his face. "I suppose this makes us even," he said slyly.

"You could say that," she replied, stepping away from the body. "Is he...?" she asked, pointing to Razzune.

"No," Jarod answered, "but if we don't get help soon I don't think he'll make it."

"Then let's get out of here," she said, bending to retrieve the laser.

Razzune was not heavy, but Jarod's progress slowed as they dashed down the hallway. Terrain disintegrators blasted the hall sending splintered door fragments flying through the air narrowly missing them. Concussions rocked the floor as they struggled to maintain their balance. Dust fumes billowed into the air giving off a choking residue.

Suddenly Quad appeared out of nowhere, like some ghostly apparition. "This way," he yelled.

Dust constricted Jarod's throat. Racked with coughing he struggled to hang on to Razzune.

"Give him to me." Quad extended his arms and relieved Jarod of the unconscious man.

Jessica squinted through the fine powdery dirt, her lungs stinging from the choking dust. "You don't know how glad I am to see you, Chief."

"The feeling's mutual," he shouted. "Now let's get the hell out of here before the whole building comes down on us!"

Jarod looked concerned. "Did Kell make it?"

"Yes, he's on his way to the portal."

The door into the dining room had been blasted open and the room stood in shambles. Portions of the slate table lay scattered in every direction. Quad paused to assess the situation. "Looks like the BorCrons got here first; they could be between us and the portal room."

Jessica stepped ahead of Quad. "Then we'll fight our way through."

Hands closed around the handle of the laser, she eased through to the connecting hallway housing the living quarters of the Eternians, her back pressed against the wall. Quad handed his laser to Jarod, who moved to Jessica's side, then Quad dropped back to keep Razzune out of harm's way.

Five BorCrons stormed out of the quarters ahead of them, their guttural voices cursing as they searched for Eternians. Jarod motioned Jessica and Quad into one of the deserted rooms where they waited, hoping the BorCrons would vacate this section of the building and leave the way open to the portal room. Suddenly a scuffle broke out in the hallway as three women were dragged from one of the rooms and roughly shoved to the floor. Two of the BorCrons aimed their lasers as the terrified women cowered before them, arms raised across their faces in an attempt to ward off what they knew was coming.

Jarod burst into the corridor and fired, killing the two BorCrons instantly. Jessica's blast hit a third man as he exited the room where the women had been hiding, spinning him around before he could take aim. Her second shot knocked him against the wall and he lay sprawled across the hallway. The two remaining BorCrons surged through the doorway, lasers firing. Jarod and Jessica fired in unison, downing both men. One of the women screamed as a BorCron fell across her, pinning her to the floor, his blood soaking her white robe. Jarod rushed to her and pushed the man off, at the same time reassuring her she was safe, as he lifted her to her feet. But she was sobbing uncontrollably. The other women rushed to her side, enfolded her in their arms, and spoke soothingly to her as she rocked back and forth.

"We'd better get the hell out of here before more show up!" Quad said, looking up and down the corridor. "We're almost there."

Razzune moaned. Jarod looked at him then Quad. "How is he?"

"Barring any more delays, I'm sure he'll make it," Quad replied. "But we'd better get there soon. He's lost a lot of blood."

The portal room door slid back and the small group rushed through just as another terrain disintegrator rocked the building, sending small pieces of ceiling scattering to the floor. Myra hurried to Quad's side as he gently lowered Razzune to the floor. "Is he...?" she asked, dropping to her knees beside the wounded man.

"Dead?" he finished for her. "No, but I suggest you act quickly."

Myra tenderly lifted Razzune's head into her lap and smoothed the damp hair back from his forehead. "I have the healing stone," she said softly, reaching into the folds of her gown. Kraft knelt beside her and placed an arm about her shoulders.

"Will he be all right?"

"Yes," she smiled up at him, tearing away the remnants of Razzune's tunic to bare the wound.

Everyone crowded around as she positioned the healing stone over Razzune's still form. As she moved the stone along the wound, the blackened shattered skin slowly took on a healthy glow and the wound began to close. Razzune's eyes flickered opened and his worn face smiled up at Myra and the others. As though they had been holding their breaths, a collective sigh issued from the Eternians. Several hands helped him to his feet, and a restored Razzune received joyous hugs from his excited fellow Eternians.

Across the room, Augueen, Condee and Retsel were gathered tight in Quad's arms. Kraft, shuffling Myra off to a corner, cupped her face between his hands and pressed his lips to hers. "I love you, Myra."

Myra's violet eyes softened, as she caressed his cheek. "And I you."

Jarod motioned Jessica aside from the others and glanced around to be sure they wouldn't be overheard. "Look, I'm as apprehensive as you are about this new planet, but judging from everything that's been happening, I don't believe we have much choice; at least for now."

Jessica frowned, shaking her head. "For all we know we might be walking into a trap."

"I believe Razzune and the Ancients are telling the truth: that there will be nothing to go back to," he answered. "Besides, Quad would never have brought his family here if he thought it was a trap."

Jessica hesitated, then glanced across the room to where Quad and his family were still huddled together. "Yes, I suppose you're right; he loves his family too much to endanger their lives." *It must be wonderful to be loved like that,* she thought. Shrugging, she smiled weakly at Jarod. "I guess I'm in no position to argue, considering we're trapped here, outnumbered by BorCrons, and the only way out is through this so-called portal. That is unless you have another idea?"

Jarod chuckled. "I'd say, that about covers it. So let's make the best of our situation and call a truce?" He smiled sheepishly. "Besides, whether you want to believe it or not, I really am a nice guy."

A slight smile creased Jessica's lips and she was about to respond when the door *whooshed* open and Kell dashed into the room, the Prophecy clutched tight to his chest. Black shielded BorCrons fired in pursuit, but the door slid back into place before they could gain access. Rapid pounding slammed against the thick steel, resounding throughout the portal room, causing panic amongst the Eternians.

Kell raised his free hand to reassure them. "By the time they are able to break through we will be gone."

Razzune stepped to his side. "Are you all right?"

"Did you think otherwise?" the Android responded, affectionately touching Razzune's shoulder. "You should know by now I'm not that easy to destroy."

Reassured that Kell was unharmed, Razzune gently removed the Prophecy from his grasp. "Thank God you were able to retrieve it," he said, gently smoothing loving fingers over the tome's engraved cover. "In all the upheaval it was overlooked, but you, my friend, did not forget."

Kell looked around and asked, "Is everyone accounted for?"

"Yes."

"Then we must go. The BorCrons will not be held back much longer." As though affirming his statement, a large portion of the door began to glow red. "They're utilizing their weapons in force to burn through the metal," he said.

He and Razzune approached the pedestal. As each placed a hand in the indentations surrounding the sphere, a swirling mass of air fill the room, then diminished. Flashes of light streaked upward and outward from the orb in streams of brilliant color, growing in intensity as everyone watched. Ribbons of color streamed into the vortex of the wormhole, swallowed in a whirlpool of motion. Anticipation filled the room as the portal to Eterna opened before them.

The pungent smell of melting steel turned heads toward the door as its center began to sag. "Quickly," Razzune urged, waving everyone towards the portal. Trembling, Condee and Retsel clung to their parents, afraid to enter.

"It's all right," Quad said, ruffling their hair. "Your mother and I are with you; think of it as a great adventure."

Myra slipped her hand from Kraft's and knelt down beside the two boys. "Your father is right," she said gently. "I know you are afraid, but *really*, it can be a great adventure; I have been to Eterna many times." Rising to her feet, she smiled up at Augueen. "It truly is a beautiful place."

The boys looked questioningly from Myra to their parents, then back to Myra. Hesitantly they reached for their parents' hands, and together the family moved to the portal. Poom peeked out from Retsel's jacket, his huge eyes alight, sensing his master's fear.

Jessica, Jarod and Kell remained until everyone was safely through. "The portal must be closed," Kell said, moving back to the pedestal. He stood for a moment looking down, then reaching out he drew the crystal stars, one by one, upward from their resting place, their glassy rods vibrating as they rose inches above the stony surface. Fixing a keen eye on Jarod, Kell plunged the rods downward with his palms. "We have thirty seconds before the portal closes."

Firing erupted into the room. "They've broken through!" Jessica yelled, backing away from the door, firing as she went. Several BorCrons surged over the threshold. Jarod and Kell returned fire; still more kept coming.

Jessica stood ready to fight, but Kell ripped her away and shoved her through into the portal. He yelled at Jarod, "We must go NOW! The portal's closing!"

The three spiraled downward into the swirling vortex of the wormhole, spinning within a kaleidoscope of churning color. When it ceased they were standing on solid ground.

"Welcome to Eterna," Kell said.

Chapter 25
Eterna

They stood on a hillside overlooking a forested valley. Fields of flowers blanketed the valley floor as far as the eye could see. In the distance snow peaked mountains rose like majestic sentinels, guarding the serene view below. "It is called Peace Valley," Kell said.

Jessica drew in a deep breath, awed by the scene. "It's even more beautiful than the pictures of Early Earth."

Kell pointed toward the horizon where a large village surrounded a castle-like structure, its gleaming spires reflecting the morning sun. "And that is Halcyon, your new home," he said, pointing to the spires. "It is named after a fabled bird that calmed the earth and brought peace.

"But there are no protective domes," Jessica said, staring off into the distance.

"There is no need," he replied. "Eterna's atmosphere is pure."

She turned to face him, suspicion etched in her eyes. "How do we know this isn't some kind of illusion you and the Ancients have created to make us *feel* safe while..."

Before she could finish expressing her doubts, Jarod spoke up. "I can answer that. It's no illusion. I remember now."

She looked at him, her brows knit together in a frown. "Then the Ancients were telling the truth; you *were* here with Kell as they said?"

"Yes, it's true, but I'm still not sure what this leadership business is about." He flashed a questioning glance at Kell who stood mutely observing them.

Jessica relaxed. "Well at least we know some of the truth anyway." She turned to Kell. "It seems I owe you an apology for doubting your motives."

Kell managed a short stiff bow. "Then if you are satisfied perhaps we can continue our journey."

Strange snorting came from the thick bush behind them. Jessica and Jarod whipped around in unison, their lasers ready to fire. "No!" Kell said gruffly. "They are harmless." He stepped into the bush leaving Jarod and Jessica casting puzzled glances at each other, their weapons ready to fire. The rustling grew more intense and they were about to go in after Kell when he appeared leading two very large beasts with ropes tied around their necks.

Jessica gasped, "What the hell are those things? They're huge." She kept her laser fixed on them.

"They are called horses," Kell said. "And they were left here for us to ride. You can lower your weapons; they are gentle creatures."

Jarod holstered his laser and walked cautiously up to one of the animals. It snorted and tossed its head. He jumped back startled. Jessica lowered her weapon and laughed. "So brave."

"All right then, let's see you touch it," he growled, stepping aside.

"Yes, well," she cleared her throat, "I will." She moved timidly toward the animal holding out her hand. It whinnied softly and pawed the ground then gently nuzzled her palm. "See," she said with satisfaction, turning her back to the animal, "there's nothing to it." The horse lowered its head and nudged her into Jarod's arms.

"Yes, you're brave, I'll give you that," he said huskily, smiling down at her, pressing her close. The response of her body spoke volumes to him as she lifted her eyes to his. Then as if he were contaminated, Jessica pushed him away and brushed herself off. Jarod chuckled, "Sorry, I thought I was rescuing you from that terrifying beast."

She glared at him. "You know, you are insufferable!"

"If you two are ready, I suggest we mount," Kell said, impatiently.

"You mean get on their backs?" Jessica asked incredulously.

"Exactly," he replied. "Unless, of course, you would rather walk. Since it is quite a distance I believe riding will be much faster. Unfortunately there are only two horses. You and Jarod will have to ride together."

Jarod smiled sheepishly. "I can ride behind you and keep you from falling off."

Jessica sneered. "No thanks, you can have the front. But first I want to see if you can even get on that...that...thing," she said, pointing to the horse. She folded her arms and waited, eyebrows raised.

"You first," he motioned to Kell.

Kell easily threw himself up onto the horse's back and nodded for Jarod to do the same.

Following his example, Jarod gripped the horse's mane and hoisted himself onto its back. With a smirk of satisfaction, he extended his hand to Jessica. She would have loved to bite it. With one strong pull she was seated behind him. Kell instructed him on how to guide the animal, and they started off.

They followed a gently sloping pathway through vineyards and trees laden with fruit. Jessica clung to Jarod as though her life depended on it, her arms wrapped tightly around his waist, her face pressed to his back. He, however, was enjoying every minute of this new experience, her nearness adding to the pleasure. They passed by a grove of peach trees and Jarod turned the horse aside for a closer look.

"So this is how they grow," he said, plucking two peaches from a high branch. He offered one to Jessica.

"Not right now," she said, clinging tighter for fear of falling off.

"Suit yourself," he responded, relishing the sweet tasting fruit.

A grazing doe and her fawn raised their heads to watch them pass. Birds nesting in nearby trees, startled at their approach, circled above their heads for a few moments then returned to settle quietly into their nests.

Jessica stared, hardly believing her eyes. "Are there more?" she asked Kell, awed that she should be seeing so many living creatures.

"These are but a few of the species that inhabit Eterna," he replied.

Halcyon's graceful spires pointed skyward, as though to pierce the very heavens. It was unlike any structure Jessica had ever seen. The walls glistened. Multicolored windows reflected the beauty of the soft countryside and well tended gardens below. As they passed beneath an archway of flowering trees her attention was drawn to a crystalline waterfall spilling into a nearby stream. Glistening rainbows billowed into the sunlit air.

The village was stirring with life. People rushed forward to greet them, laughing in their excitement, hands reaching up to touch them. Marketplaces overflowed with every variety of fruit and vegetable imaginable, all new to Jessica who had never seen anything like them except in the Archives of Ancient History. The fragrance of flowers hung in the air, their sweet scent a marvel to her senses. Young women in pastel robes stood waving. Everyone was shouting, "Welcome. Welcome." Some of the women threw flowers at the mounted trio. Men in long white tunics with colorfully striped sashes draping gracefully to their sandaled feet, cheered and waved their caps. Jessica looked down at her gray uniform feeling drab amid so much beauty. A small child scampered up offering Jessica a flower. She smiled down at the child and gladly accepted it, lifting the bloom to her nose to breathe deeply its sweetness.

Razzune, Kraft and Myra were waiting for them as they brought the horses to a halt at the base of the steps to Halcyon. Myra and Kraft stepped forward to greet them.

Kraft was laughing. "You look ridiculous up there, pal."

Jarod mumbled something under his breath, then lifted a leg over the horse's neck and slid off. Kraft slapped him on the back. "Well done."

Smiling up at Jessica, who sat nervously alone on the horse, Kraft chucked. "I gather this was not the greatest experience you've ever had." Myra poked him in the ribs.

"Never mind him," she said to Jessica. Turning to Jarod, she added, "I believe Jessica could use some help." Kraft started forward, but Myra frowned at him.

"Oh, yeah," he said slyly, clearing his throat, "Jarod, help the lady down."

Cautiously Jessica slipped her foot over the horse's back and Jarod lifted her easily off the animal. She placed both hands on his shoulders as he slowly let her body slide down his before setting her on her feet. She was sensuously aware of his hands on her waist and leaned into him, her eyes questioning. It was all he could do to control his desire to kiss her then and there, but too many eyes were fixed on them. He held her close for a moment then gently put her from him. Jessica looked disappointed. Jarod almost said aloud, *You can't continue to hide your feelings, Jessica. You want me as much as I want you.*

Embarrassed by the silence surrounding them, Jessica turned to Razzune. "Where are Quad and Augueen? Did they make it safely?"

"Yes, they are fine and have retired to their rooms. The boys were exhausted and their mother felt they should rest. Quad said they would join us later."

They climbed the wide stairway and entered a great hall, much like Sanctuary. But where Sanctuary had been void of color, Halcyon was alive with it. Scarlet drapes lined the massive windows facing the gardens. Miniature replicas of galaxies, stars and worlds filled the ceiling above their heads, slowly rotating in quiet splendor. Red velvet couches and chairs surrounded a huge open fireplace in the center of the room. Gold-carpeted staircases bordered each side of the hall rising to the landing above.

Jessica turned slowly taking it all in. She hadn't realized until now how sterile New Earth had been with its computerized life. Even the air they had breathed was created by giant computers centered within the core of each colony, keeping everything and everyone alive by artificial means.

"I gather you are pleased?" Razzune asked, his eyes alight with pleasure. "Halcyon is your home now, yours and Jarod's."

Jessica looked long and hard at Razzune. "Yes, this is a beautiful place, but whatever gave you the idea I intend to live here with Jarod, or he with me? You've taken a lot for granted, Razzune, you and the Ancients." Her eyes drew away for a moment as though in thought; when she looked at him again, her voice was sad. "I realize now the Ancients were telling the truth and New Earth is facing destruction." She bit her lip and looked away struggling with her emotions. "I could have saved Legend if only I hadn't remained at Sanctuary."

Razzune placed his finger beneath her chin and turned her to face him, his look sympathetic. "Don't blame yourself, Jessica. There was no way you could have made it past the BorCrons. Legend would not have wanted you to sacrifice your life for his. You must begin a new life here with Jarod."

Jessica touched his arm, her voice low. "I know you mean well, and I appreciate your kindness, but I have no intention of becoming someone's idea of a perfect wife." She nodded towards Jarod who was talking with Kraft and Myra. "I'm sure there must be a more suitable female among the Eternians who would be happy to marry your new leader. Now, if you don't mind, I'm tired and would like to rest."

Razzune smiled. "Yes, of course, I'm sure Myra will be happy to show you to your room."

Razzune watched as Jessica approached Myra. The two women talked for a moment, then headed up one of the staircases to the landing above and disappeared from sight. Kell excused himself from Jarod and Kraft and spoke to Razzune out of their hearing. "I'll begin preparations."

Chapter 26
Revelation

Razzune sighed and moved across the room to converse with the two men. Nearing them he overheard Kraft say in an irritated manner, "That's your problem; bullheaded as usual. She's..." Spying Razzune out of the corner of his eye, he mumbled, "Never mind, I'll take it up with you later." Turning, he smiled and clapped Razzune on the shoulder. "Eterna is all you said it would be. I understand there is also an art gallery and library."

Razzune nodded. "It is the Ancients' desire that you enjoy every aspect of Eterna. Many of the things you have seen, the animals for instance, and food, grown in our own orchards, were recreated after their own planet, Trykona. Early Earth, in its beginning, was a place of harmony and peace much like Trykona, before humans in their struggle for power, destroyed it. They simply want for us that same peace and harmony. The worlds surrounding New Earth are once again in upheaval throughout the galaxy: planet warring against planet, each greedy for controlling power." Razzune looked hard at Jarod. "That is why you were chosen to be our leader."

Jarod started to interrupt, but Razzune lifted a restraining hand. "First hear me out." Jarod tensed but nodded in affirmation. Razzune lowered his hand and continued. "The Ancients waited many years before choosing you, Jarod. They brought you here as a young man, and under Kell's tutoring, trained you for that leadership. You have been gifted with great power."

Jarod laughed. "Power? What power? I have no idea what you're talking about." Then he turned to Kraft and chuckled. "Oh, I see; they think by telling me I have some kind of super power I'll be convinced I'm their leader." Then turning back to Razzune, he said, "Nice try, but I'm not buying it. You'd be better off with Kell; he fits the image better than I do."

"Very well," Razzune said, smiling, unaffected by Jarod's disbelief. "We shall see. Now there is the matter of the chip I gave you. Do you still have it? You risked your life to save mine and I shall be eternally grateful."

Jarod searched his pocket. "I entirely forgot about it." Extracting the small chip, he turned it over several times in the palm of his hand, before handing it to Razzune who stood waiting. "If you don't mind my asking, why is this so important?"

A serious Razzune clasped his fingers over the chip. "You will see in time." Then his face took on a cheerful look. "But for now, my friends, we should rest and prepare ourselves for this evening. The Ancients will join us, and I believe your questions will be answered."

"Where have I heard that before?" Jarod mocked.

Kraft nudged him. "When are you ever gonna take this seriously?"

"Okay, I'm as anxious to hear what they have to say as you are," Jarod responded, "but I'm still skeptical."

***

One of the great windows to the library stood open. A gentle evening breeze fluttered the drapes and the scent of flowers drifted in from the gardens. Razzune led the small group into the large comfortable library.

Jessica marveled at the stacks of books rising from floor to ceiling. Jarod and Kraft moved from shelf to shelf pulling out volumes, examining their titles. Myra smiled at Kraft's childlike enthusiasm.

Quad and Augueen joined them; their sons, Condee and Retsel, were left in the competent hands of one of the Eternian women. "I've never seen anything like it," Augueen commented, turning to Quad. "Have you?"

"Only in the Archives of Ancient History. But that was small in comparison to this."

"There must be thousands," Kraft said in awe.

"Yes, I do believe so," Razzune responded nonchalantly, his hands clasped behind his back.

Myra chuckled, delighted with their reactions. "I knew you would be surprised." She pointed to the stacks. "Many such books were destroyed by Vantra in his quest to dominate. He ruled that computers should be the source of all knowledge. Of course, his 'Age of Enlightenment' being the criteria. The Ancients desire is that Eterna be free of such evil."

Jarod moved to one of the many chairs stationed around the room, and dropped into it. "I've yet to understand why they want me?"

Kraft and Myra joined him, while Quad and Augueen continued to browse through the library. Augueen ran her fingers over one of the sturdy tables, touching it as though it might have a story of its own to tell. Kraft took the chair at

Jarod's side, and Myra contented herself to sit on the arm of his chair, her arm draped across his shoulders. Jessica wandered about the room a moment longer then selected a chair across from theirs. Leaning forward, she asked Razzune, "You said the Ancients were going to tell us what we want to know. Just when do they intend to do that?" Her voice held an edge to it. "We've rested, eaten, and viewed this marvelous library, but I don't believe that's why..." She stopped in mid sentence as a pinpoint of light distracted her.

All eyes turned to the expanding orb as it grew brighter, faded, then grew brighter again, the Ancient's features accentuated in the illuminated sphere. Silence weighed heavy as the small group waited for them to speak. Steel gray eyes surveyed each in turn, as though reading their minds. Satisfied, they spoke, their synchronized voices almost gentle. "It is good that you are assembled together. You reached Eterna safely, but it will not be easy to adjust to such different surroundings as you have known on New Earth, or Borkia," they added, addressing Quad and Augueen who had selected chairs near the others. "Although there is no lack of technology on this new world, still you will find the simplicity of life a challenge. We have created for you a place much like that of our own planet Trykona, filled with new life and abundance of food from the soil."

The Ancients centered their attention on Jarod. "The time has come for you to know why you were selected to rule Eterna. Your grandfather, Kardon Faus, was Trykonian. When the Saroaks invaded our world, he was enslaved along with the others and taken to their home planet. Many years later he managed to escape aboard a cargo ship to New Earth. The Trykonian length of life was far greater than you can imagine and he was still a young man. Sadly, however, Kardon was the only Trykonian to survive Saroak captivity.

He took as wife a New Earthian woman; your grandmother. She was unaware of his true origins.

"Three years after he was selected Prefect of New Earth, Bardas Vantra, greedy for power, had him assassinated, and bestowed upon himself the greater title of Prince. Since we could not save New Earth from *his* tyranny, we could at least save the people known as Eternians and create for them a new world. We selected your father to rule, but before we could reveal our secret to him, he too was killed in a Federation skirmish. Only you were left, Jarod. You are what remains of our race and therefore must assume leadership of Eterna."

Incredulous, Jarod sprang from his chair and stared up at the Ancients. "Are you inferring I'm part alien?" He couldn't believe what he was hearing. Suddenly aware of Quad and Augueen's eyes on him, he quickly apologized. "Sorry, I meant no offense."

"None taken," Quad responded, taken by surprise himself.

Clearly agitated, Jarod brushed a hand through his hair. "You must be mistaken!"

"If you did not possess our ancestry," the Ancients replied, "you would never have been chosen. You will find your grandfather's name written in the Prophecy as well as your father's and your own. Only one who is Trykonian has the power to rule."

"Then why don't you?" he snapped.

"Our mission has been accomplished; our time is at an end."

"And if I don't wish to rule?" Jarod responded, teetering between disbelief and anger. "What will happen?"

"At this very moment the Asteroid has entered New Earth's gravity." The steel gray eyes seemed to penetrate Jarod's very soul. "Nothing will remain. Without a leader,

Eterna will cease to exist as well, and all those living here will be dispersed throughout the galaxy to other planets. Eterna can exist only under a Trykonian leader."

The words fell like a blow, hard and brutal. Jarod stiffened as he assessed the enormity of the situation. The others sat in stunned silence. Addressing the Ancients, he asked simply, "How long do I have to make my decision?"

"You have until dawn," was their brief reply. Then their sphere rose to the ceiling and vanished.

Without so much as a glance at the others, Jarod turned and stalked from the library.

What an awful responsibility to carry, Jessica thought, watching him go. "What do you think he'll do?" she asked Kraft.

Kraft looked up at Myra sitting on the arm of his chair, then his eyes met Jessica's. "He'll do exactly what he should. He can't help himself. That's just the way he is." Kraft smiled ruefully. "The poor sap."

Chapter 27
Destruction

A sullen Prince Vantra, having returned to New Earth, sat slumped in the Seat of Knowledge in the Council Hall; his robe draped about him like a protective shield, his cruel features twisted in hatred. Jessica Caldar had slipped through his fingers and the new world was now beyond his reach. Even the execution of the incompetent fools who let her escape hadn't brought him satisfaction. He raised his head and slammed his fist down hard on the arm of the chair. *Damn them all to hell! Gone only a few days and already the power mongers are fighting for control!* He feared his hold on New Earth was weakening. *Even some of my staunch allies are threatening to break from the Federation. And the people, blast them, are beginning to grumble!* Vantra jerked to his feet and started pacing. *All it takes are a few discontents to stir them up. I've been too easy on the troublemakers. It's time I made examples of them!*

He moved down the stairs to the vid-screen to initiate the order, but before the first words were out of his mouth several men burst into the hall. Vantra whirled around, eyes blazing with fury. "What do you mean breaking in here like this!" He was outraged. "Guards! Where the hell are my guards!"

"Please, Your Highness," one of the men said breathlessly, stopping long enough to salute, "you're in danger! We're all in danger! We've come to take you to the Glennden. The Asteroid has suddenly veered off course and its trajectory is bringing it into direct contact with New Earth. It's imperative you leave now!"

Vantra whipped his robe about him and glared at the man. "I was assured the Asteroid was nowhere near us. Now all of a sudden I'm to believe that for no reason it has changed course?" He shook his head violently. "Mars base is mistaken. I'm not going anywhere!" Pointing a finger at the door, he bellowed, "Now get the hell out of here before I call out my BorCrons!"

The lieutenant persisted, knowing that at any moment he might be a dead man, but he had to convince his leader. "Sire, the Federation has already confirmed the situation and launched rescue ships. The colonies are evacuating at this very moment!"

Vantra slowly mounted the stairs to the Seat of Knowledge and collapsed into it. Leaning forward, looking down at the men, he pointed a finger at the lieutenant, his voice steely. "Someone is lying to you, Lieutenant. The Federation wouldn't launch ships without notifying me or my Council! Now get out!"

The men looked at each other, marked fear on their faces. The lieutenant bowed stiffly, his voice wavering but persistent. "Sire, your Council has already left on one of the rescue ships."

Vantra stormed down the stairs, his eyes grinding into the lieutenant's. The man took a step backward, cringing, thinking Vantra meant to strike him, but the blow never fell.

Vantra's arms were pressed to his sides, his face contorted in anger. "How dare they abandon me! They'll pay with their lives, the bastards! Call my guards!"

The lieutenant swallowed hard, his fear intensifying. "They've deserted, sire."

Vantra cursed again and again, his breath coming in short bursts. "Cowards! All of you, cowards!" he bellowed, his hands knotted into fists. "I'll have you executed!" It was more than the lieutenant and his men could take; they broke ranks and fled, leaving Vantra to his own fate.

He couldn't believe what he was seeing. Never had anyone dared turn their back on him. Stalking up the stairs, he sat heavily in his chair, bewildered, shaking with rage.

As the men fled out the chamber door into the street a wall of sound burst upon them. Panic saturated the air. People were running, screaming, clutching whatever possessions they could carry. In the distance evacuation ships were being launched. Stations were swamped with masses of people fighting for position to be transported up to the rescue ships.

Balls of flaming fire streaked across the evening sky lighting up Bostonia's protective shield. Occasionally one would smash into the dome, and like sunspots, flare high into the night sky.

Increasing in frequency, each strike grew more intense. The dome shook, vibrating the ground.

The Asteroid slammed full force into New Earth, collapsing the integrity of all her colony's shields. Vantra cried out as the floor beneath him shook violently throwing him out of the chair onto his knees. A shattering boom tore through the chamber, sending the marble statues crashing from their platforms. Vantra looked up, horror etched across his face, his hands raised, as tons of debris buried him alive. A strand of white hair fluttered up through the dust, then disappeared beneath a deluge of marble as the building collapsed inward.

New Earth's magnetic fields gave way, shutting down all life sustaining computers. Microwaves tore through the fabric of her core, draining gravity, knocking the planet off its axis. Explosions tore through the atmosphere, as billions of particles billowed into space, flaring like fiery comets.

Then, as though an invisible vacuum sucked them back again, the particles reassembled themselves and New Earth novaed into bright luminosity, birthing a new star.

Chapter 28
Restoration

Razzune addressed Jessica. "There is something you must see. Kell is waiting for us in the laboratory."

"Laboratory?" she repeated. "You have a laboratory here?"

"Yes, of course," he replied matter-of-factly. "We have many such labs throughout Eterna." He looked at the others. "Perhaps you would care to join us?"

Everyone welcomed the diversion. "This should be interesting," Kraft said. Looking suspiciously at Myra he added, "And I suppose you knew about this as well?"

"Yes, of course," she smiled sheepishly, taking his hand.

"Women," Kraft sighed.

Razzune moved to the end of the stacks. "Computer. Lab." With quiet precision the shelves slid back and he motioned everyone through. They entered a well-equipped laboratory, its brilliantly illuminated room spotless. Vid-screens and computers took up a portion of the floor space. Two padded tables, surrounded by laser probes, stood within a glass-enclosed chamber near the entrance. Kell rose from one of the computers and acknowledged their presence with a brief nod.

Kraft whistled. "Wow!"

Kell motioned everyone to a row of seats facing a raised platform used to project holograms. "You have the chip?" he asked the old man.

Razzune stepped to the platform. Taking the chip from his pocket, he inserted it into the projection mechanism. Compassion etched his aged features as he turned to address Jessica who remained standing. "Before the hologram begins, Jessica, you must know that your father was aware Vantra would do everything in his power to discover the portal to Eterna. He feared for your life and that is why he built Legend, to advise and protect you. I deeply regret I must be the one to tell you he was discovered by Vantra's BorCrons and destroyed during a search of your quarters."

Jessica was shocked. Tears glistened on her lashes. When she spoke her voice shook with emotion. "Legend was all...I...had." A sob escaped her throat. "If only I had returned to New Earth, I might have been able to save him."

Augueen moved to her side and gently laid a hand on Jessica's arm. "I'm so sorry, Jessica. I don't know who Legend was, but it's obvious he meant a great deal to you."

Quad looked puzzled and asked Razzune in a low tone, "Have I missed something? Who was this Legend?"

"Let us view the hologram first," Razzune said. "Then if Jessica is up to it perhaps she will answer whatever questions you may have concerning him." Razzune turned to her. "Would you like a few more moments?" he asked, concerned.

"No," she answered, squaring her shoulders. "Go ahead."

Augueen returned to sit with Quad. She smiled weakly at him then turned her attention to the platform.

Razzune began the hologram.

Jessica inhaled sharply as her father's image appeared. Moving close, she pressed her hands to the platform's surface, staring intently into her father's eyes. He was as she remembered him: The patch of thinning hair she had smoothed down so often when he couldn't be bothered with his appearance, the weary smile hidden beneath the gray mustache that flowed into his short goatee, and the bright, intelligent eyes, always serious yet ready to crinkle up in a smile whenever she teased him. She reached out as if to touch him. So concentrated was she on his beloved features she missed his first words.

"...you will know Legend has been discovered or destroyed."

Jessica listened intently, not budging, fearing his image might disappear if she made the slightest move.

"...I programmed him to send this hologram on to Kell. If that should happen, Kell's instructions were to contact you and decipher the information I have coded into this message. Everything is there to rebuild Legend, like himself, in human form..."

Jessica's hand flew to her mouth. "Oh my God," she whispered aloud. "Is it possible?"

"...He will be the same friend you've always known." Ryden hesitated a moment as though making a decision then continued. "There is one thing more, Jessica. Something I should have told you long ago when you were growing up. But I felt it was a decision you alone should make when the time came. The Ancients told me about Jarod Krinner, the young man chosen to be leader of Eterna. They asked that I pledge you to him, but I could not in all good conscience make that decision for you even though I knew it to be right..."

"Well I'll be dammed," Kraft chuckled, whispering to Myra. "So those two *are* meant for each other."

Jessica stared at her father's image in disbelief as his message continued.

"...I knew his grandfather well. Trust your heart, Jessica." Ryden's image began to waver and fade. "I know you will make the right decision." The hologram vanished and the platform was empty. As empty as Jessica felt that moment.

"And this Legend is...?" Quad asked, looking from Jessica to Razzune.

"A computer of artificial intelligence," Razzune replied, sensing Jessica's need for silence at the moment. "But much more than that." His eyes softened as he nodded in Jessica's direction. "Legend was more than a computer to her. He was her friend."

Chapter 29
Persuasion

Jessica stood poised by her bedroom window staring down at the gardens below. Like prison bars, slivers of early dawn threaded their way across her rumpled bed. Making her decision, she threw on the silk robe draped at the foot of her bed and cautiously made her way out the door, her quick steps taking her down the hallway to the winding staircase.

Sleep had been impossible. Her father's words kept thrashing through her mind over and over again. *"The Ancients wanted me to pledge you to Jarod." I wonder what Jarod will say to that,* she thought, questioning her motives for even caring what he thought. Gripping the edge of the curtain, she crushed the velvet between her fingers. *Admit it, Jessica; you'd like very much to know.*

She slipped through the library door into the fragrant scented garden just as the first golden glow of dawn streaked the morning sky. Sensing she wasn't alone, she turned to see Jarod standing nearby, a hard set to his jaw marring his otherwise handsome features. He was obviously deep in thought. There was no way to avoid him unless she ducked into the rose bushes. *I'll be dammed if I'm going to let him intimidate me*, she chided herself, standing defiantly waiting for him to discover her there.

Jarod's thoughts were on the decision he must make. *How can I let the Eternians be scattered throughout the galaxy when it's within my power to give them their own planet?* Frustrated, he brushed a hand through his dark waves. Turning, he spotted Jessica watching him, her gown a halo of white accentuating the outline of her slim body. Her hair hung loose about her shoulders framing her beautiful face in auburn highlights. His eyes devoured her.

Realizing too late how scantily dressed she was, Jessica's cheeks burned. She wished she could flee back to her room, but there was nothing for it now but to stay put. "I'm...I'm sorry if I've disturbed you," she stammered.

Jarod smiled and dropped his gaze. "I gather you weren't able to sleep either?"

"Yes. I mean no," she answered, correcting herself. *Dammit, why does he always make me feel so awkward!*

"Care to talk about it?" he asked, motioning her to a stone bench close by.

"I hardly think my problems are worth discussing, you have enough of your own right now," she answered, irritated with him for probing her weaknesses. She started to turn away, but he reached out and gently placed his hand beneath her elbow.

"Then let's discuss mine."

Jessica looked questioningly at him, but seeing his expression, nodded. "All right, that's the least I can do considering the circumstances."

He sat, motioning for her to join him on the bench. She waited quietly for him to speak. Jarod rested his elbows on his knees and folded his hands in front of him. Glancing sideways at her he began to speak, doubt evident in his tone. "I really don't know if I'm the right person to lead these people. Training or not, it's a responsibility not to be taken lightly." He straightened up and smiled weakly at her. "The simple truth, Jessica, is that it scares the hell out of me."

For the first time she realized his vulnerability. He always seemed so sure of himself. This was a side new to her and she felt her pulse quicken. "There's no simple answer is there?" she said softly. "You're the only one who can make that decision. The Eternians trust you, Jarod." She turned and looked at him her eyes tender. "I know I do."

His next statement caught her off guard. "Enough to share it with me?" He moved closer, strumming her cheek with the back of his hand. "You must know by now how I feel about you, Jessica. I'm through playing games."

She looked into his eyes. "I...I...," was all she could say.

Jarod rose and pulled her into his arms. "Say yes, Jessica," he whispered, his breath warm on her cheek. "With you by my side the doubts won't seem so immense."

The granite-like resolve that had kept him at bay dissolved and her arms went around his neck. Jarod lowered his mouth to hers and her body strained against him. She felt the throbbing beat of his heart merge with hers. Jarod cupped her face between his hands and looked deeply into her green eyes. "I take it that's a yes?"

"Yes," she laughed breathlessly, happiness flooding through her like quicksilver. He loved her. "Oh yes," she repeated, burying her head in his shoulder.

She felt his body shake and looked up. Jarod was chuckling, his eyes bright as he said, "I can just see the look on Kraft's face when he finds out you're in love with me." Turning serious, he held her out at arm's length. "You are in love with me, aren't you?"

"Of course, I have been for a long time," she said, kissing him passionately. Then looking sheepishly she chuckled, "However, I doubt it will come as any great surprise to Kraft or Myra." Her lips sought his again and he locked her in his embrace. She wished that time would cease its motion and this moment would never pass.

Epilogue

Jarod had left several days ago to meet with the new Federation of Planets and the days for Jessica seemed to pass in a fog. Kraft and Kell were away too. As Eterna's principal ambassadors, they were often gone for weeks. She wondered if Myra missed Kraft as much as she missed Jarod. *You'd think after ten years together, his absence wouldn't leave such a void in my heart,* she thought. *Since the fulfillment of Eterna's Prophecy, our cities have become major trade centers. Jarod has worked so hard, too hard,* she mused. *The planets are at peace because of his timeless efforts. How much can one man be expected to do?* Melancholy was shaking her resolve to never complain. *I miss him so.*

Sighing, she glanced at the silent man by her side and asked, "What are you thinking, Legend?"

"I think, Jessica, it is good to be here with you."

She smiled and turned to look towards Peace Valley. "Do you think he's happy there?" she asked.

The two were standing on one of Halcyon's balcony's overlooking the valley beyond where Razzune's resting place lay.

"I know he is," Legend said, reassuring her. "It was his desire after all."

"Yes," she sighed, "I just wish Jarod could have been here for the ceremony; he was so fond of the old man."

"As were all of us," Legend replied, his dark brown eyes intent on her.

Jessica never understood the process by which Kell had brought Legend to life, but oddly he appeared exactly as she thought he would. She knew her father's DNA had been programmed into restoring him and that was probably why certain of his actions were so familiar. She studied his strong intelligent face. Where Kell's complexion was pale, almost translucent, Legend's skin had a warm hue to it. His hair was dark brown and long, pulled back tightly from his face with a leather strap. The Eternian guard uniform fit his muscular frame handsomely. All in all, Legend was an impressive figure.

"Have I something on my face?" Legend asked seriously, touching his cheek.

"No," she laughed, "I was just thinking how dear you are to me."

"You know, Jessica, when I was a computer, you never said that."

A twinkle lit her eyes. "When you were a computer I didn't need to."

Shrieks of laughter rose from the garden below. "What are those rascals up to now?" Jessica said, peering over the balcony. A breathless Myra stood below. She looked up and pointed to the hedged garden. "Your sons are playing the evil Vantra again," she hollered up. "Condee and Retsel went after them but they've made their escape into the dark caves of Pragora. My brave Aurora says she will find the evil princes and take revenge on them just like her Aunt Jessica did."

Jessica hollered back, "Tell her to show no mercy." She turned to Legend. "What say you? Shall we join the fray?"

Legend frowned. "The last time I went after your two sons they managed to tie a rope across the path." He rubbed his shoulder. "I still smart from the fall."

Jessica laughed and patted his arm. "Legend, those boys adore you. They would never hurt you purposely. And they *did* apologize. C'mon," she challenged, waving her arm in the air for him to follow as she flew down the hall, robe billowing out behind her. Taking the stairs two at a time her laughter could be heard echoing throughout Halcyon. "Wait for us, we're coming."

THE END

Fay Smith
penladyfay@comcast.net

Printed in the United States
68889LVS00005B/61-123